DIAMONDS AND RECEPTION

A VERITY SPARKS MYSTERY

DIAMONDS AND DECEPTION

SUSAN GREEN

WALKER
BOOKS

First published in Great Britain 2016 by Walker Books Ltd
87 Vauxhall Walk, London SE11 5HJ

10 9 8 7 6 5 4 3 2

Text © 2011, 2016 Susan Green
Cover artwork © 2016 Nina Tara

This book has been typeset in Perpetua

Printed and bound in Great Britain by Clays Ltd, St Ives plc

British Library Cataloguing in Publication Data:
a catalogue record for this book is available from the British Library

ISBN 978-1-4063-7173-4

www.walker.co.uk

For Helen Green
(1924–2008),
who invented teleagtivism

1

LADY THROTTLE'S HAT

My name is Verity Sparks, and I've got itchy fingers. The Professor calls it teleagtivism. Sounds like a disease, doesn't it? But it's not. It's more like a talent. A gift. I've always had it, but I didn't know I had it until the summer of 1878. It happened the day I finished the yellow hat.

The hat was mostly feathers, with one poor little bird left whole and stuck onto the brim.

"Like a dead duck on a plate, ain't it?" I said as I held it up.

Madame sighed. "Yes, it is. But it's what she asked for. Oh, dear!" She fussed around on the workbench for a few seconds, and then sighed again. "My spectacles, dear – have you seen my spectacles?"

I whisked them out from under a bundle of ribbons.

"And my scissors?"

I found them too, and handed them to her with a yawn. It was half after eight on a Saturday morning, and Madame and I had been working by lamplight since a bit after five. Madame was my employer. The gold letters on the shop window said:

Madame Louisette
Boutique de Modiste à la Mode

That's "fashionable hat shop" in French, but to tell the truth, Madame was about as French as a Chelsea bun. Her real name was Louisa Splatt.

"But I couldn't call the shop 'Splatt's Hats', now, could I?" she told me when I first started with her. "It just don't have no *chic*."

Madame had four of us apprentices living in. Emily and Bridget were sixteen, and Beth, my special friend, was thirteen like me. We got a wage besides our board and lodging, and though she had a way of boiling all the taste out, Cook gave us big helpings, and she didn't mind us girls having the odd bit of bread and cheese when we got hungry. Most days we worked only ten hours, with Sundays off and a half-day holiday every month. Madame was a kind employer, and so we counted ourselves lucky.

The other girls were working quietly, cutting and

stitching silk linings, and Miss Charlotte, our saleslady (Madame called her the *vendeuse*) was downstairs arranging a new window display in the shop.

"I'd be lost without you, dear," said Madame.

"Well, your scissors and your specs would be," I said. "Now, into the hatbox?"

Madame sighed yet again. "How many hats has Lady Throttle had so far?"

"She took two with her on her first visit and one last week. This is the fourth." I crumpled tissue paper and packed it around the bonnet.

"She hasn't paid me a penny. That bird came from South America, ordered in special. And I owe the wholesaler ... where's the bill, dear?"

"Here."

Madame looked at the bill and her saggy old face sagged even more. "Oh my gawd! How am I going to pay that?"

Hats weren't an easy business. Madame had to pay the factory in Southwark for the hat forms, and the wholesalers for trimmings and silks, and then there was wages, rent, food and coal.

"It'll turn out all right, you'll see." I gave her a brief hug. "Lady Throttle wanted the hat before ten o'clock. Shall I go now, Madame?"

"Yes, dear. Her address is..." Madame peered at

her own scrawl in the order book, "... number three, Collingsby Square. Do you know where that is?"

"Yes, I do." I'd been running messages and making deliveries for so long it seemed like I had a map of London inside my head.

"Well, off you go." Madame gave me an absent-minded smile and then began patting at her face in mild panic. "Where are my specs? I've lost them again."

"They're on the table, Madame."

"So they are. Bless you, dear."

I was halfway down the narrow stairs when I heard a call.

"Verity! Are you there?" It was Miss Charlotte. It was funny, but it almost seemed like she'd been waiting for me. "Did Madame give you money for your fare?"

"No, Miss Charlotte. It's only twenty minutes' walk."

"But it might rain, and the hatbox will get wet. You had better catch the omnibus."

It wasn't like Miss Charlotte to be so thoughtful, and I must have glanced at her curiously, for she continued, "I'm sure Madame would wish it. Those hatboxes cost a pretty penny." She handed me sixpence. "Bring back the change, won't you?"

"Yes, Miss Charlotte." I went to put the coin in my pocket but she stopped me.

"You'll lose it like that. Here." As she handed me a little drawstring purse made from red silk brocade, she suddenly gave a big smile. If I hadn't known better, I'd have said she liked me. "I made it myself. You may have it to keep."

"Why thank you, Miss Charlotte," I said, but I was puzzled. A present from Miss Charlotte? She was usually as sour as vinegar with us young ones.

"Off you go then," she snapped. That was more like her.

Fashionable ladies don't get out of bed till after ten, so the streets near Madame's were quiet and I could glance into the shop windows as I hurried along. Not for the likes of me, of course, but a cat can look at a king, and I looked at lace and fine linen handkerchiefs, perfumes and French soaps, umbrellas and parasols and leather travelling cases. In the jeweller's shop, a pair of white-gloved hands were reaching through the curtains with a velvet tray of rings and gold chains. The florist was taking delivery of roses and violets with the dew still on them, and in the confectioner's (this was the one I liked the best) the shop girls were piling boxes of toffees, jujubes and bonbons on the counter. One of them smiled at me and gave a friendly wave. I waved back. After a morning hunched over in the workroom, it felt good to be out and about. The omnibus, a double-decker carriage pulled by ten horses, rumbled past, but I didn't bother trying to catch it. Miss Charlotte was wrong about the weather. It was a perfect day.

Lady Throttle's house wasn't hard to find. It was in a quiet street lined with trees, smack-bang in the middle of a row of tall white buildings with lots of columns and arches and fancy iron railings. I went down the narrow steps to the tradesman's entrance and rang the bell. I rang again. And again. I hesitated a bit, but time was getting on, and Lady Throttle had been most particular about the time. She wanted to show her new hat to Sir Bertram before he left for the city at ten.

"Ruddy hell," I said to myself (pardon the language). "Here goes." And I ran up to the front door and lifted the knocker. It was loud enough to wake the dead, and seconds later a uniformed maid no older than me opened the door. She took one glance and decided she needn't waste her manners.

"What?"

"A hat from Madame Louisette for Lady Throttle,"

I said. I peered past her into the entrance hall. It was all white marble and gilt mirrors and shiny furniture.

"So you've come to the front, have you?" She put her hands on her hips. "The tradesman's entrance not good enough for you?"

"I rang and no one came."

"As if I haven't got enough to do, but I have to jump up and come the very second some—"

"Violet! That's enough." A tall woman dressed in plain black came briskly down the stairs, and Violet just melted away.

"I am Crewel, Lady Throttle's personal maid." She beckoned with one long bony finger. "Come with me. No, not up there!" She waved me away from the marble staircase. "We will use the service stairs."

The service stairs were for the servants. They were dark, narrow and steep, covered with threadbare carpet. The usual, I thought. Good enough for the maids, even though they might catch their heels and break their bloomin' necks falling downstairs. But when I followed Crewel into Lady Throttle's dressing room, I was surprised to see worn carpet there too, and faded curtains. A bit shabby, really, for all it was so flash in the hallway.

"Sit there." Crewel pointed to a stool in the corner, and then she turned to the lady sitting at the dressing table. "The girl's here with your hat, m'lady."

Lady Throttle ignored me, and that way I got a good look at her. She was very small and pretty, with black hair, white skin and bright blue eyes. She was posed in front of her mirror like a fashion plate in one of those magazines Madame got sent from Paris. Showing off her dress, I thought – and there was a lot to show. It was red, ruffled and flounced and I guessed there was close to ten yards of silk braid on her bustle. A bit too smart for a hat delivery on a quiet morning in her own house.

After a while she spoke, but not to me. "Crewel," she said, in a slow, drawling voice. "Give Bertie this." And she held out a folded piece of notepaper.

I sat and waited with the hatbox on the floor beside me while Crewel left the room for a bit. Humming a little tune, Lady Throttle patted her cheeks, licked her lips and smoothed her hair, and then she just sat looking at herself in the mirror until Crewel came back. She was followed by a tall, fat old gent. Was this Sir Bertram, Lady Throttle's husband? I stood up and bobbed a curtsey, but he too ignored me.

"Dear, dear Bertie," said Lady Throttle in a caressing voice, standing on tiptoe to kiss him.

He smiled and pinched her cheek. "Here we are then, puss," he said, taking a small blue velvet case from his breast pocket. She held out her hand.

"No, no," he said. "Let me." He took something glittering out of the case and pinned it to her dress.

"I shall wear it tonight, Bertie. Will you be proud of me?" she asked. He gave a long, happy sigh by way of reply, and then turned to leave.

"Wait, Bertie. Won't you look at my new hat?"

"Of course, my love."

Crewel clicked her fingers, and I brought the hatbox forward.

Lady Throttle took the hat out and settled it on her curls. "Isn't it lovely?" she asked, but instead of agreeing, Sir Bertram clutched his throat. His face went purple and his moustache began to quiver. I thought his eyes were going to pop right out of his head.

"Put it back," he gasped.

"What's the matter, Bertie dear?"

"Feathers…" He held his nose with one hand and waved the other around helplessly. "Feathers… Allergic…" he wheezed, and staggered out of the room.

"Well, well, well." Lady Throttle took off the hat and let it drop to the floor. "So I shan't have my yellow bonnet after all." She gave a little laugh, and then turned to me. "Come here, girl. What is your name?"

15

"Verity Sparks, ma'am."

She looked me up and down, and smiled. I didn't quite like that smile.

"You'll have to take this hat back, and get me another one instead."

"There's nothing else in yellow at the moment, ma'am—" I began, but she cut me off short.

"Who said yellow? Something white, I think ... red and white, to suit my new afternoon costume. Something that will set off the brooch. See?" She unpinned it from her dress and held it out in her hand. "This is the famous Throttle diamond. Bertie's great-grandfather took it."

Did she mean he'd stolen it? I didn't know what to say, so I said nothing.

"He took it from the eye of an Indian idol. Just snatched it out and rode off with it. How cross all those natives must have been."

More than cross, I thought.

"It's worth thousands of pounds," she continued dreamily. "Isn't it beautiful?"

Beautiful? I hadn't seen too many diamonds, not up close anyway. "It's very sparkly, ma'am," was the best I could do.

"Those stones around the edge are rubies. See how they twinkle."

"Yes, ma'am." Sparkly and twinkly was all very well, but my business was bonnets. "Madame Louisette has something in ruby satin, ma'am," I said. "With white silk ribbons."

"That will do." She put the brooch down on her dressing table, and stood up. "Bring it back this afternoon. At three o'clock."

"Yes, ma'am."

I was surprised. Lady Throttle had made such a fuss about the feathered hat – she'd been fussy about everything she'd ordered – and here she was leaving the choice to me. Still, she was paying the bill. Or would soon, I hoped, for Madame's sake. I turned to go.

"Come back, Verity."

I did as I was told.

"Hold out your hand and shut your eyes."

Why? I thought, but I obeyed.

She moved towards me and stood so close I smelled her perfume. Lily of the valley, it was. "Hand me my purse, Crewel."

I heard Crewel's skirts rustle, and she brushed against me, and then Lady Throttle pressed something into my palm. "There," she said. "For your trouble."

I opened my eyes. It was a chocolate.

"Thank you ma'am," I said, and curtseyed.

I don't like chocolate.

The bell jangled as I opened the door to the shop. Miss Charlotte frowned slightly, but she didn't stop talking.

"The blue bonnet is charming, ma'am," she purred. "But I feel that you are one of the few ladies who could do justice to this more unusual shade."

Unusual shade! It was like mouldy cheese. A customer had ordered it to her own design and then returned it. Madame had promised Charlotte a bonus if she could flog it off to someone else.

Which she did. I waited while Miss Charlotte wrote out the bill with a smile just like the cat that got the cream. She looked up when I put Lady Throttle's hatbox on the counter.

"What's this?" She pointed to a dirty streak on the pink-and-white paper.

"Mud, Miss Charlotte. I had to walk back. The omnibuses was full up."

"You should have taken more care, Verity."

"Sorry, Miss Charlotte. Anyway, Lady Throttle doesn't want it. All them feathers give Lord Bertram the sneezes."

"Sir Bertram," she corrected me. "He's a baronet, not a lord."

"Yes, Miss Charlotte. That red bonnet with the white ribbons, is it still here?"

She pointed to a hatbox on the shelf.

"Could I have it, please? It's for—"

"Lady Throttle. I know." She handed it down to me. "Next time," she hissed. "Don't come in through the shop. The customers don't like it."

"No, Miss Charlotte. I mean, yes, Miss—"

"You haven't lost that purse?" she interrupted.

"No, I—"

"Go and have something to eat," she said. Again the smile. "You can pick up the hatbox on your way out."

2

A CONFIDENTIAL INQUIRY

I was at the tradesman's entrance right on three o'clock, and this time Violet opened the door on the first ring. Crewel arrived a few seconds later, and gave me a funny kind of smirk.

"You are very punctual," she said, and since I didn't know what that meant, I just bobbed a curtsey and followed her upstairs.

Lady Throttle was standing in front of the fire. She'd changed from the flashy red into a pale blue dress. Very sweet she looked, almost girlish. I curtseyed and tried to hand over the hatbox, but she shrank back like I had lice.

"There she is," she cried, pointing.

I looked behind me. "Beg pardon, ma'am?"

"You wretch! Where is it? I demand to know. Where is it?"

"Please, Lady Throttle." A tall man with a big

brown moustache loomed out of the corner. "Do not distress yourself, ma'am. Allow me to question the young person."

"She has it. I can tell. Guilt is written all over her wicked face. And to think..." Lady Throttle pressed a lace handkerchief to her eyes. "To think that I gave the vile creature a *chocolate*!" She sank into an armchair and began to weep quietly.

"Sit over here, if you please." The man indicated the stool I'd perched on that morning. "You may put the hatbox down," he added kindly.

I'm not slow on the uptake, and I could see where this was leading. Someone had nicked something. And they thought that someone was me. Bloomin' hell!

"My name is Saddington Plush," the man said. He was quite a young man, maybe just turned twenty in spite of the moustache, with curly brown hair and kind green eyes. "I am a confidential inquiry agent, and Lady Throttle has called me here today, in great distress." He paused, and she let out a long, shuddering sob. "Let me take down a few details." He whipped a little notebook and a pencil from his top pocket.

"Your name?"

"Verity Sparks, sir."

"The name Verity," he said, looking down at me

all serious and stern, "comes from the Latin *veritas*, and it means 'truth'. I hope you intend to be truthful, Verity?"

"Yes, sir," I said. Pompous ass, I thought.

"Your age and employment?"

"Thirteen, sir. I'm an apprentice trimmer at Madame Louisette's."

"Who are your parents?"

"Thomas and Elizabeth Sparks, sir."

"Where do they live?"

"They're dead, sir."

"We don't need her pedigree," interrupted Lady Throttle. "Search her."

"Just a few more questions." He turned back to me. "After your parents died, where and with whom did you reside?"

"Beg pardon, sir?"

"Who took you in?"

"Auntie Sarah and Uncle Bill."

"Tell me about your uncle and aunt, Verity."

"They run a used-clothes stall. Auntie Sarah couldn't keep me, and so I got apprenticed to Madam Louisette."

"When did you last see them?"

"Christmas time, sir." Only for a few minutes though. Auntie Sarah had a black eye, and that meant

Uncle Bill was back on the grog. I didn't want to cause any trouble, so I'd given her a quick kiss and gone away.

Lady Throttle stamped her foot, and Mr Plush turned to her. "There is method in my questioning, as you will see. What is your uncle's name?"

Oh, no, I thought. So this is where Mr Plush was leading. "Bill — I mean William — Bird, sir."

"Aha!" Mr Plush got out another notebook and flipped through the pages till he found what he was after. "Just as I thought," he said. "Are you aware, Verity, that he is a notorious fence?"

Lady Throttle was wide-eyed. "A fence? Whatever do you mean, Mr Plush?"

I tried to look as blank as a sheet of paper, but I knew. We used to have visitors, lots of them, coming at all hours with parcels and packages for Uncle Bill. Money changed hands, no questions asked, and then they'd go away. So I knew about Uncle Bill all right, but I wasn't going to tell Mr Saddington Plush.

"No, sir," I lied. "He's an honest man, he is. He's no fence."

"Fence is thieves' slang for a receiver of stolen goods, Lady Throttle," he explained.

"Stolen goods." Lady Throttle was shrill. "A rookery of thieves! A den of criminals! Thank God we were not all murdered." She shot me a glance that'd poison a snake. "It is all clear to me now."

"Verity Sparks, I propose to you that you have stolen Lady Throttle's brooch, with the intention of passing it on to your uncle, the notorious fence, William Bird. What do you say to that?"

"I say I haven't done it, sir." I tried to speak loud and strong, but I felt like a rat in a trap, and it came out as a whisper. They're fitting me up, good and proper, I thought. *Who done it?* That bony old maid, Crewel? I stole a glance at her, and she met my eye, cold as an icicle. Then again that little smirk. Something was going on.

My fingers began to itch. It was annoying, and I rubbed them together, but it only got worse. They were stinging now, worse than a wasp bite. What was wrong with them? Lady Throttle was saying something but I couldn't hear what it was. The only thing I could think of was my itchy fingers, and then...

"The brooch is in Lady Throttle's purse," I gasped. All eyes turned to the embroidered bag on her bureau.

Lady Throttle almost fell off her chair. "What nonsense."

"It is," I insisted. In a flash I'd seen it, clear as day.

24

Mr Plush turned to Crewel. "May I have Lady Throttle's purse, please?"

"You may have no such thing, Mr Plush!" Lady Throttle was red in the face. "This creature is simply trying to delay the inevitable. Search her, sir!"

"Crewel?" Mr Plush held out his hand.

Mistress and maid locked eyes, and I saw Lady Throttle give a tiny shake of her head.

"Surely, Lady Throttle, if there is any chance of a mistake?" pleaded Mr Plush. "I know that a lady such as yourself would not wish to falsely accuse this young person, however dubious her ancestry."

My what? Never mind that. Grabbing my chance, I snatched up the bag and handed it to Mr Plush.

His hand hovered over it. "I need your permission, Lady Throttle."

"Which I do not give," Lady Throttle snarled. For a pretty little thing, I thought, she can come up ugly all right. "Hand it over, and *search the brat.*"

Mr Plush bowed. "Of course, Lady Throttle." But somehow, in the handing over, he fumbled and dropped it, and out onto the threadbare carpet rolled a hair comb, three gold-wrapped chocolates, a couple of sovereigns – and the Throttle diamond.

"My God!" cried Lady Throttle. "Crewel, you idiot. Why did you not tell me you'd put it in my purse?"

"I ... I..." stammered the maid, and dodged as Lady Throttle threw a small clock at her. A silver hairbrush and a cut-glass perfume bottle followed, then Lady Throttle flung herself into the armchair and began drumming her heels on the floor like a child having a temper tantrum.

"You'd best go," said Crewel sourly, and opened the door.

I couldn't get out of there fast enough. I hurtled down the stairs and into the hall. It was empty, but when I opened the front door I nearly collided with the master of the house. Sir Bertram looked down at me with surprise.

"What's this?" he said.

I pushed past him and ran as fast as I could.

"Hey, you!" I heard him shouting, but I was down the street and round the corner already.

I ran for fifty yards, then I sat in the gutter and up came my lunch. After I'd retched a few times I just sat there, trembling. My hands were still tingling, ever so slightly, and I held them out in front of me and stared at them.

Itchy fingers. That had come first. And then suddenly, with no shadow of a doubt, I'd known where the brooch was. It had been like a picture in my mind's eye, clear and sharp and certain and sure. But there was no way I *could* have known that the brooch was in the purse. It was true I'd always been good at finding things, but not like that. And I'd never before had itchy fingers.

"Miss?"

I wiped my mouth with the back of my hand and stood up. Mr Saddington Plush gave a quick bow.

"Miss Sparks, I——"

I backed away from him. "*Miss Sparks* all of a sudden, is it? What do you want with me? I ain't going back there."

"No one wants you to go back there, Miss Sparks," he said. He was puffing slightly. "I simply wanted to apologise."

"What?"

"Say sorry."

"Why should I say sorry? I never done it. It was the maid, Crewel; I saw her put the brooch in the bag."

"No, you didn't."

I stared at him.

"How did you know where it was, Miss Sparks?"

"I dunno what you mean."

He sighed. "Have it your own way," he muttered. He fished in his inner pocket, brought out a little rectangle of pasteboard and handed it to me.

"It's my card," he said. "I'd like to discuss this matter with you further. At your convenience. Feel free to contact me. Any time."

I glanced at it.

Saddington Plush and Son, Con—

Continental-something-or-other. I popped it in my pocket and turned to walk away.

"Let me detain you just one instant further, Miss Sparks," he said. He took my hand and folded it around a couple of coins. "If you continue along this street, and then turn left, you will be able to find a cab for your journey home."

Never take money from a gentleman, Cook had warned me. Evil designs, she said. But I was too tired to walk and too tired to care about designs, evil or otherwise.

"Thank you, sir," I said.

"I shall expect to see you, Miss Verity Sparks."

Expect all you like, Mr Saddington Plush.

Even with the cab ride, it was after five by the time I got back to Madame Louisette's. I went to the kitchen first, and Cook gave me a couple of fairy cakes. I wondered, as I ate them, what to say to Madame. Any kind of trouble with customers was bad for business, and I knew she'd worry when I told her.

She knew already. The door of her private parlour was open and she was sitting at her bureau with a glass in her hand and a gin bottle in front of her. A litter of bills and letters and advertising fliers lay mixed with ribbon samples and odd trimmings around her on the floor, as if she'd simply swept the lot from her desk. She'd been crying.

"Oh, Verity." She swayed to her feet. "Verity, I'm so sorry. So very sorry, my dear girl."

"What's the matter, Madame? Have you heard about the brooch?"

She nodded.

"But you know I didn't take it."

"I know, I know." She gulped down the rest of her gin and poured another half-glass, then scrabbled around on the floor for a piece of paper. "But here. Look! It's a note from Lady Throttle. She insists I let you go."

"What do you mean?"

"Kick you out. Get rid of you. She says that if I don't, she won't pay her bill."

"Is it so very much?"

Madame ignored me. "And she'll tell all her friends not to pay. Don't you understand, dear? If they don't pay me, I can't pay for these." She tossed a bunch of ribbons into the air. "And then they'll send the bailiffs round. I'll be ruined."

I sat shocked and still while Madame continued drearily, "And not just me: there's Emily and Bridget and Beth, and there's Charlotte, and Cook as well. I'll have nothing."

I could see why Madame was scared, but my heart sank like one of Cook's fairy cakes. Where would I go? What would I do?

"I'd like to stick up for you, Verity, I truly would, but she's got me, and there's nothing I can do." Madame upturned the gin bottle and shook the last drops into her glass. "Nothing."

3

GOODBYE TO ALL THAT

Three days later at eight o'clock in the morning I was out on the street with my shabby old carpetbag. I glanced back at the shop. For more than two years Madame Louisette's *boutique* had meant home and friends as well as my job. My room with Beth; Cook's stories and second helpings and rough, kind hugs; Madame's little lost things that I was always finding ... well, goodbye to all that, I told myself. If I thought about it too much, I'd cry or get scared. With a wave to Cook and Beth, who were leaning out of the third-storey window, I started to walk as fast as I could down Oxford Street.

I was hoping that Auntie Sarah could put me up for a couple of nights until I found somewhere to live. Cook said there were always rooms at Ma Bolivar's. It was a respectable place, she told me, adding to watch out for lice because Ma Bolivar packed, racked and stacked her boarders four to a room. I thought of Beth and the cosy attic we'd shared, and sighed.

I'd need a job first. Madame had given me a letter addressed to her old friend Miss Musquash of the Belgravia Dress Agency. She bought and sold high-class used clothes, and employed a few girls to mend and freshen up the trimmings. I'd have to work day and night to earn a wage, and Madame knew it, for she clutched me to her bosom and snuffled.

"I wish I could do something, Verity. I wish I'd never laid eyes on Lady Throttle."

Me too.

The smell hit me first. It was nearly three years since I'd lived with Uncle Bill and Auntie Sarah, but the smell of their market stall brought it all back. Their tiny house in Racketty Lane, only a couple of streets away, was always crammed with merchandise, and every room stank of musty, greasy, sweaty, worn and worn-again old clothes. Not to mention the overflowing drains, the piles of rubbish and empty beer bottles, and the stale fat from Uncle Bill's favourite pork sausages.

And speak of the devil, there he was. Uncle Bill was lounging in front of his stall with a line of silk handkerchiefs hanging like sad flags above him.

"Is Auntie Sarah about?"

"Wotcher want 'er for?" He spat a gob of phlegm that just missed my shoe.

"I've lost my place."

I shouldn't have said it. I knew straightaway I shouldn't have. He came right up to me and stuck his face so close to mine that I could see every broken vein and gin-blossom on his nose. "Lost yer place? And so you come crawling back here? Auntie Sarah will help you, is that it? Well, little Miss Fancy-breeches, you know what? You know what? Yer Auntie Sarah don't exist."

I stared at him.

"She don't exist." He grabbed one of the handkerchiefs and waved it around in the air. "Tra-la-la! Yer got no auntie at all."

Was he joking? Or had he gone barmy? Then a terrible thought came to me. "She's not … not…"

"Dead? 'Course she's not dead. I 'aven't told her she can die yet."

I was bewildered by now. "Then what do you mean?"

"What I mean, missy, is this. She don't exist because she's not yer auntie."

"I don't understand."

Uncle Bill must have got tired of talking in riddles.

"She's not yer auntie because yer a foundling," he said. "A dirty little bastard of a foundling."

My jaw dropped and Uncle Bill laughed. He was enjoying this.

"When you was only a few months old someone wrapped yer in a blanket and left yer in a box in Seacoal Lane. And who found yer? Lizzie Sparks. And what does she go and do? Not give yer up to the foundling 'ospital like anyone else would. She adopts yer."

Finally, what Uncle Bill was saying sunk in. Ma and Pa were not my real parents. I was that shocked and surprised, I came over all giddy. I leaned against the trestle table, just staring at him. Could it really be true?

"I'm adopted?"

"Ain't that what I jist told yer? Yes, full of the milk o' human kindness, my sister-in-law," sneered Uncle Bill. "But I'm not, so 'op it."

"But Auntie—"

"Yer got no auntie. Yer got no uncle. Throw yerself on the parish, go on the streets, starve in a gutter – I don't care." He gave me a long, slow look, full of hatred. "Don't come 'ere again, or I'll knock yer teeth out. And that's jist for starters." He jabbed my chest hard with his finger. "See?"

I nodded. "I see."

I wasn't staying there the night, then. Better try Ma Bolivar's.

As I walked, I kept thinking about Uncle Bill's thunderbolt. Was it true? *Was it true?*

I rolled that question round and round my mind like a marble in a jar. Uncle Bill had always hated my guts, and it'd be just his style to make something up on purpose to hurt me. But still I wondered. You see, I had a bit of a mystery packed in my carpetbag.

Pa died first. He got the typhoid fever, and Ma nursed him so well it seemed like he was getting better. But he didn't. Then Ma took ill. Most of the time she didn't even know me, but near the end she came to herself again, and I could tell there was something troubling her. I asked her did she want the minister, but she shook her head.

"The lucky piece," she whispered. "The ring ... in my chest of drawers. In brown paper."

"Here, Ma. I've got it." I showed her the parcel, and she breathed a bit easier.

When I opened it, I found a little quilt, a ring and an old coin. I'd never seen them before; Ma had never so much as mentioned them.

"Keep them safe," she said. "They're your future

and your fortune." But I never got to find out what she meant, for she took a turn for the worse. She passed on soon after.

Uncle Bill sold everything, even the canary. I did ask myself whether Ma meant that I should sell those things too. The ring was real gold and the quilt was the finest fancywork, made of coloured silk in a pattern of stars. But in the end I never so much as showed them to Auntie Sarah, even though Uncle Bill raised the roof about the expense of keeping me. I hid them under a loose floorboard. I didn't have anything else to remind me of Ma, and I never thought any more about how she'd come to have them. But now I wondered, if Ma had lived a bit longer, would she have told me.

I sighed, wiped my eyes, and looked around me. I must have been in a bit of a daze, because I'd walked for half an hour in the wrong direction.

"Bloomin' hell," I said. My feet were already aching. I turned around and started plodding back in the direction of Ma Bolivar's.

Ma Bolivar would want some rent in advance, of course. Madame had given me some money to tide me over, and I'd put it in that red purse that Miss Charlotte had given me. I'd put the purse in my carpetbag, but I suddenly thought, what if it got stolen? I'd be sunk. There were snatch-and-grab artists everywhere. How easy would it be to yank the bag out of my hand and run off with it? The thought made my blood run cold. I took the purse out of my bag and slipped it into the pocket of my dress, where I could feel it bump against me as I walked.

Then I started to worry about pickpockets. It would be just as easy for someone to jostle up against me on the crowded street. I left a few small coins in the purse, but the rest of the money I wrapped up in my handkerchief and stuck down the front of my bodice. It made a funny lump on my chest, but with my shawl pulled round me, no one would notice. I felt a lot better after that.

I was hungry by then, so I stopped at a pie stall. When I reached into my pocket, I found Mr Plush's card. Not on your life, I thought, and dropped it in the gutter. But when I fished a penny from my purse to pay for the pie, I brought something else up too. Something tiny and hard. I blew the fluff off it.

"Gawd, what's this?" I whispered to myself.

It was bright red and sparkled. It was just like one of the tiny rubies from around the Throttle diamond. And it was right here in my purse.

I thought back to Lady Throttle's dressing room.

She'd made me shut my eyes when she'd put the chocolate into my hand, and she'd been so close I'd smelt her perfume. Crewel was right behind me. She could have put it in my purse then. But why? Lady Throttle had been determined to make trouble for me. She'd insisted that I be searched.

Oh. Now I understood: it was so that Mr Plush would find the ruby, figure that it had come out of its setting, and use that as evidence.

The pie turned to sawdust. They didn't transport convicts any more, but I'd get prison. No question about it. Cook loved to read the news aloud to us of an evening, and I knew all about Holloway Gaol. No one would believe I hadn't done it, especially with my precious Uncle Bill being so famous.

I stared at it. Horrible thing, winking like a little bloodshot eye. Quickly, I unbuckled my carpetbag and thrust it in among my clothes. Then I wondered if I should even keep it. Maybe I should just throw it in the gutter, like I'd thrown Mr Plush's card. I started to rummage in my bag, but just then, out of the corner of my eye, I saw him again – a young man in a stovepipe hat, clean-shaven, very tall and sort of spindly in the legs. I'd first spotted him a few streets back, and I realized what I should have known for the last half-mile. I was being followed.

Who was he? What was he up to? I had the funny feeling that I'd seen him before, but I'd be blowed if I knew where. I walked on, and so did he. I stopped, pretending to tie my bootlace, and he stopped too. I crossed the road. He crossed the road. How was I going to get rid of him? I turned a corner quickly, then ran like the blazes to the next street, crossed it, and looked back. He was nowhere to be seen. Feeling pretty pleased with myself, I trotted along happily until I heard my name called. It was a girl's voice. She was halfway down a lane, standing in the shadows, a small skinny creature with a cloud of yellow hair. I didn't recognize her, but walking the streets of London delivering and picking up orders, I'd met all sorts. How could I remember every one?

"Verity!"

"Do I know you?"

"Verity, do come quickly."

"What's the matter?" I asked, starting forward. I was so intent on her pale face and trembling voice that I didn't notice someone coming up behind me. The first I knew about it was when a hand was clapped over my mouth. For an instant I was too surprised to move, but then I jerked my head and bit down hard on the hand. My attacker yelled and I wrenched myself free just long enough to see it was a man. Then he gave me a clout to the head that made me see stars. Before I could run or shout or anything, he shoved a rag into my mouth and rammed me against the alley wall with my hands twisted up behind my back.

"Come on. What you waitin' for? Check 'er pockets."

I felt the girl close to me, felt her hands on me. I tried to kick her but my skirt got in the way.

"Cut it out, you bloody little fool," he said, and then he pushed me face down in a puddle.

I was more mad than scared. How dare they pull a trick like this in broad daylight? I lifted my head up, spat the rag out of my mouth and yelled, "Help, thief!" as loud as I could.

"Get the bag. Quick, someone's comin'."

"Hey, you!" A new voice. I tried to stand up but got a boot between my shoulderblades.

"Run!"

There were footsteps and then more footsteps coming from another direction and heavy breathing and a few confused yells and then a *thwack* as something hit something else. Flesh and bone, I guessed, 'cos there was a yelp of pain and a lot of swearing.

"After him, Opie."

I could hear them running away now. Was it over? I lay there, winded, tasting blood and dirty water.

Then two hands picked me up and set me on my feet. I blinked up at my rescuer.

"Are you injured, Miss Sparks? Any bones broken?"

It was the young gentleman in the stovepipe hat, the one who'd been following me. He bowed slightly, and handed me a grubby pasteboard card.

"You dropped this, Miss Sparks."

I looked again. "Where's yer moustache?"

Everything was moving and swaying, just slightly, and creaking. There was a strong smell of leather and the sound of horses' hooves. I stared at Mr Plush – for that was who it was, without the moustache – and he smiled. "You're quite safe, Miss Sparks."

"Safe," I repeated dozily, and then I sat up in alarm. I saw trees and tall fences and paved footpaths. Where was he taking me? "Never go with a member of the male sex in a carriage or a cab," Cook had told us girls. Evil designs again. Was this a kidnapping?

"And this is Mrs Cannister," he continued, gesturing towards a plump middle-aged lady sitting next to the window, half asleep. She had a red wool scarf wrapped around her head, and her face was bruised. She nodded, smiled and said something like, "Mumf, mumf, humf," and I remembered how I'd been bundled into the carriage, and this lady had wrapped me in a shawl and given me a drink from a silver flask. Elderberry cordial, Mr Plush said it was, but there must have been more than elderberries in it. It put me straight into a doze.

"Mrs Cannister is our invaluable housekeeper," he explained. "When I took her into town today to the dentist, I thought I should also like to continue our conversation, and so I called at Madame Louisette's. She told me you had left her employ that very morning, and that you were going to Mrs Bolivar's boarding establishment. So I followed you."

"Lucky for me," I said. "Thank you, sir."

"It was a pleasure, Miss Sparks. You are safe and sound. And here is your bag, as well."

"My bag..." Dirty and muddy, but safe. I fumbled around in it until I found the ruby.

"Look," I said, holding it out to him. "It must have been put there, sir."

"Planted," he said. "And probably fake as well." He solemnly wrapped it in his large white handkerchief. "Hmmm. Miss Sparks, you have been, as they say, set up. You realize that you'd most certainly be before the magistrate if that little gem was discovered in your possession?"

I nearly lost my temper. "I ain't stupid, sir."

"I wasn't suggesting you were. I promise you that

you are perfectly safe from prosecution, but I would like to ask you to assist us in our inquiries. Believe me, this Throttle affair interests us very much." He paused. "Will you tell me now how you knew that the brooch was in Lady Throttle's purse? Was it a form of mentalism?"

I gawped at him.

"What I mean is, did you notice any tiny clues in Lady Throttle's behaviour? Did her eyes almost imperceptibly flicker towards the purse? Did she perhaps move her hands?"

"My fingers started to itch," I said.

You should have seen the look on his face. "*Your fingers started to itch?*"

"They itched something dreadful, and then I saw where the brooch was, like a picture in a book, but sort of inside my head. And my fingers ... well, they sort of..." I stopped. It did sound silly.

"Have you had itchy fingers before? I mean, when you were looking for something?"

"No, sir."

"But you think that feeling the itch and finding the brooch were definitely connected?"

"Yes, sir. Well, I don't really know, sir." Now I was confused. "I'm just good at finding things," I said lamely.

"I know. Madame Louisette told me. She'd already mislaid her spectacles and a packet of bugle beads when I called this morning."

"That'd be right, sir." I laughed. "But you know, half the time I find what she's lost before she's even missed it. She says I've got the gift."

He was gazing at me with a funny expression, half pleased and half not.

"A gift for finding things?" he said softly.

"I s'pose so."

"And itchy fingers." He shook his head, and went on in a different voice. "We are nearly at Mulberry Hill, my family residence."

I stared out of the window. The carriage turned through two high brick gateposts into a gravelled drive that led through trees and grass and more trees, but I couldn't see a house yet.

"Nearly there," said Mr Plush.

We rounded the last curve in the drive, and stopped in front of a white house with a verandah and a little tower and a climbing rose reaching almost to the third storey. It stood among garden beds, all by itself, with enough space around it to park a dozen omnibuses.

"You live here? You must be—" I stopped myself from saying "rich as a platter o' gravy", for I knew

44

that wasn't manners. I'd seen grand houses before, of course, when I was out delivering hats, but never one with so much garden and so many trees and so much … well, space. It was like a palace.

"Welcome to Mulberry Hill, Miss Sparks," Mr Plush said as he helped me and Mrs Cannister out of the carriage.

A black-and-white spaniel came tearing around the corner of the house and stopped in front of me, panting.

"And Amy welcomes you too," said Mr Plush.

I wasn't much used to dogs. When I kneeled to pat her, straightaway she licked her big pink tongue, sloppy as a wet washcloth, right across my face.

"That's enough, Amy! But it's a good thought. Miss Sparks, when we get inside, I suggest you may like to freshen your attire before we partake of a little refreshment."

I stared at him. I think my mouth was open.

"What is it, Miss Sparks?"

"You talk like a book, sir."

"I read a lot of books, Miss Sparks." He grinned. "But I don't have to talk like this, you know. It's a kind of habit, caught from my father. You'll see when you meet him. I'll rephrase. Would you like to have something to eat?"

I nodded.

"And have a wash and change of clothes?"

"What for?"

"Because, Miss Sparks, to speak plainly, you smell."

4

MULBERRY HILL

The maid's name was Etty, and she showed no surprise at having a muddy apprentice milliner come in through the front door. She led me up the stairs with a friendly, "This way, miss."

"What's that?" I said, staring, when she opened the door for me. I'd never seen anything like it.

"It's the bathroom, dear," she said (no more "miss" now we were alone, but she spoke kindly for all that). "The hot water gets heated up in this here gas geyser –" she pointed to a big cylindrical tin drum sort of contraption – "and goes down a drain once the bath is finished with. No carrying cans of hot water up and down stairs in this household," she added proudly. She turned a tap and, just as she said, steaming water gushed out.

"Strip off then, dear."

"What?"

"So you can have your bath. Pooh! These do smell. Soaked through, they are."

I hesitated. The truth was, I'd never had a bath in my life. A jug and basin and a washcloth was all I'd ever known.

"I'll leave you to it then, shall I?"

I had my bath. The geyser burped and belched, and I was scared the ruddy thing might explode, but mostly I enjoyed it. I never knew you could feel so clean. Halfway through, Etty bustled in with my carpetbag.

"D'you want me to lay your clothes out?" she asked.

I shook my head. "I don't need no one to wait on me," I said. "Thanks all the same," I added, in case she thought I was rude.

"Suit yourself, dear." She shrugged her shoulders and smiled as she shut the door. "I'll come back in a tick."

There was a mirror in the room, and after I dressed, I looked at my reflection. I sighed. My dress was a hand-me-down of a hand-me-down, and you could tell. In this house, with everything so clean and neat and even the housemaid done up like a lady, I felt very shabby. Never mind, I told myself, you won't be here long.

There was a knock and Etty walked in. "You finished? Good girl. Give us your bag then, and I'll take it to your room."

"My room?" I grabbed the bag out of her hand. This was what Cook had told me about – respectable-seeming men and women who lured young girls just like me into their clutches. I held the bag to my chest.

"Have it your own way," said Etty, and then a smile twitched the corners of her mouth. "You know, dear, you're safe as houses."

"We'll see," I muttered.

"Come on, then. Come with me. They're waiting for you in the library."

Library? I didn't want to seem ignorant so I didn't ask.

It turned out to be a big room full of books. I never knew there were so many books. Books from floor to ceiling, and ladders so you could reach up to the highest shelves. Books the size of suitcases and tiny books in glass-fronted cases. Neat rows of books all matching in red and gold, and then shelves all mixed with fat books and skinny books and books of different colours. In the middle of the room there was a round table, piled high with newspapers and letters and, yes, more books. At the table sat Mr Saddington Plush and another gentleman. They both stood up when Etty, with a friendly nudge, sent me into the room.

"Miss Sparks," said Mr Plush, smiling. "Allow me to present my father, Mr Saddington Plush, senior."

I knew before he told me that it must have been his pa, for he was the spit and image of him, only a little bit stooped and the brown hair turned to grey. His moustache was real.

"Good day, Miss Sparks," he said, taking my hand and bowing over it in an old-fashioned way. "I must thank you for giving up your valuable time to assist us in our inquiries. Won't you have a seat? And I shall ring for tea."

He beamed a smile at me, but all I could do was stare. Tea? He was asking me to have a cup of tea with them? At the same table and all? Didn't he know I was just an apprentice milliner?

Young Mr Plush shoved a gluepot and some scissors and a pile of newspaper clippings out of the way. "Here we are," he said kindly, and then whispered, "It will be all right, Miss Sparks. Don't worry."

Worry? *Worry?* I was beside myself. What were they up to, bringing me all the way out here? And as to staying the night – well, the idea! But how was I going to get back to Ma Bolivar's? Would Mr Plush send me back in the carriage, or put me on a train?

He'd have to pay my fare, I reasoned, since he'd taken me to wherever this was. I shoved my bag under the chair and sat down, very stiff and awkward, just as Etty and a younger girl came into the room carrying trays.

"Ah, tea!" said Mr Plush senior, as if it was a surprise. After all, it was him that had rung the bell. He lifted the lid of one silver dish. "Anchovy toast." And then the other. "Teacakes." He rubbed his hands together. "*Bon appétit*, Miss Sparks."

"Beg pardon?"

"He hopes you're hungry," said young Mr Plush.

Well, I was, and they were as well – those gentlemen really could tuck it away – but after we'd taken the edge off with toast, cakes and tea, Mr Plush senior got down to business. Very serious, he was.

"Miss Sparks, on Saturday we thought that Lady Throttle had made a silly mistake. Today, we realize that she has attempted to use us for her own purposes, and we don't like being used. We don't like being treated as fools. And we most especially don't like seeing an innocent person hurt by the selfish machinations of others. Is that not right, SP?" Without waiting for an answer, he went on. "Lady Throttle has made a grave mistake, my dear. She mistook my son's youth for naivety and thought

51

she could use him to blame you for the theft of the brooch. When her plan went awry, she sought revenge by getting you dismissed. Perhaps she thought that no one would care what happened to a milliner's apprentice, but we do, and we would like to see justice done. Do you understand?"

I nodded. It was a lot of words, but I got the sense of it.

"Miss Sparks, since we feel in some way responsible for your regrettable predicament, we would be honoured if you would stay with us until we have — what is your term for it, SP?"

"Cracked the case," he said, grinning. "You see, Miss Sparks, I don't always talk like a book."

"Mrs Cannister you have already met, but my daughter Judith and my sister Mrs Morcom reside here at Mulberry Hill as well, so you will have no lack of female chaperones." He twiddled with the ends of his moustache. "And there's Etty and Cook and Sarah and little Jemima, the scullery maid. Females galore, in fact."

I added them up in my head. A housekeeper, a cook, two maids and two ladies made six in all. It seemed Etty was right. I would be as safe as houses.

I bobbed a curtsey. "I would be very happy to stay, sirs. Thank you very much."

"And I believe, Miss Sparks, that you may be able to help me." Mr Plush senior beamed that lovely smile at me again.

"Help you, Mr Plush?"

"SP tells me you are very good at finding things. Your employer, Madame Louisette, swears by you. My son tells me that you attribute your discovery of the brooch to itchy fingers." I could feel myself blushing. I searched Mr Plush senior's face for signs that he was laughing at me, but he seemed perfectly serious. "May I ask you to put your powers to the test?"

"Do you mean you've lost something, sir?"

"My meerschaum."

"Pardon?"

"My favourite pipe. Meerschaum is a clay mineral, hydrous magnesium silicate, and often used to make ornamental pipe bowls."

"I see." I didn't quite.

"Meerschaum is German for sea foam."

My fingertips began to tingle, ever so faintly. And then I did see. I had a kind of picture inside my head, but not of sea foam or clay or even of a pipe.

"Is there a purple silk cushion in the house?" I asked. "With tassels?" My fingers were really itching now, and I found myself heading for the door.

"With or without tassels, I have no idea," said Mr

Plush senior. He gave me a curious look. "Why do you ask?"

With the two of them following, I went down a corridor, through a set of doors and down another corridor. More doors. "I think it's in here," I said.

"But I never smoke in there. Almeria would have my hide. Ah well, Miss Sparks, if you say so." He opened the door for me.

Once again I didn't know what kind of a room to expect, but I tell you now what I wasn't expecting. A snake! Thick as a drainpipe and so long that it was wound twice round the potted tree in front of us and draped three feet on either side.

I stifled a scream. "It's a ... it's..."

"She's a diamond python," said Mr Plush senior. "*Morelia spilota spilota*. Her name is Cleopatra." He smiled and stroked her, and she reared up so that her head was level with his. "Beautiful isn't she?" he said admiringly. "Pure muscle. I say, Miss Sparks, are you all right? You're awfully pale."

"It's ... it's..." Another snake. On the floor. Right near my foot.

"That's Antony," said young Mr Plush.

Suddenly Antony stirred. His tongue flickered out, and for the first time in my life, I fainted.

5

TELEAGTIVISM

I opened my eyes to see two faces hovering above me. Two ladies' faces. One was old and looked like a pug, and the other was young and looked like an angel.

"How are you feeling, dear?" said the angel, placing a cushion behind my head.

"Fuss and bother," said the pug. "Antony's about as dangerous as an old sock."

"Here's a glass of water," said the angel, putting it to my lips while I took a sip. "Are you overheated? Would you like me to fan you?"

"Of course she doesn't need a fan. There's no point coddling her," said the pug. "Healthy young girl like this should be up and about, not languishing on a sofa."

"I'm very sorry, Miss Sparks." Another face hovered into view. It was young Mr Plush.

"As am I, Miss Sparks." The voice of Mr Plush senior seemed to come from somewhere inside a tree.

"Where am I?" It looked like we were in the middle of a forest. "And where are the ... the..." I looked around for the snakes.

"Antony and Cleopatra are back in their case. Where they should have been all along," the angel said sharply. "You know all the servants are terrified of them, Aunt. It was very thoughtless of you. Down, Amy!" The black-and-white spaniel I'd met when I arrived jumped up and tried to lick my hands.

"Fiddlesticks," said the pug. "There's nothing the maids enjoy so much as a good fit of hysterics. Besides, I was sketching them *au naturel*. Well, as *au naturel* as you can get in a suburban conservatory."

"Conservatory?" I said.

"We're in the conservatory," said the angel. I had no idea what she was talking about, but she explained. "It's where we grow our rare and tropical plants. That's why it's so warm. And the snakes live in here too."

I gazed around me. Of course it wasn't a forest. It was a big room all made of glass, with a tiled floor and raised garden beds and large pots for the plants and trees. A fountain trickled water. The trees were called palms, I learned later, and there were about twenty different kinds. I was lying on a wicker sofa, and near by were two wicker chairs, a dog basket and a table laid with tea for two. The spaniel, the angel, the pug and the snakes must have been having a tea party when we walked in.

"Since Papa and SP are so forgetful, I'll introduce myself," said the angel. "I am Judith Plush."

Miss Plush had the family resemblance all right, except her hair was more chestnut than brown. She had melting dark eyes and the same beautiful smile as her father and brother. No moustache, of course.

"A thousand pardons, Judith my dear. Where are my manners?" said Mr Plush senior. He turned to the pug. "Miss Sparks, this is Mrs Morcom, my sister. Almeria, this is Miss Sparks. She is helping us with some inquiries."

"How d'you do?" said Mrs Morcom and held out her hand. It was bright green. "Don't worry about that," she said, seeing my surprise. "It's viridian. One of the more permanent pigments. It's the hydrated oxide of chromium that does it."

"Yes, ma'am," I said, bewildered.

Mrs Morcom was shorter than me, but somehow her deep, croaky voice made her seem bigger than she was. So did her fierce, bristling eyebrows. And her hat. In the millinery trade I've seen lots of hats, but never one like this. It was a kind of turban, a foot high, made of shiny purple silk with a tasselled fringe hanging down the back. She looked like she had a cushion on her head.

"Oh."

"Are you in pain, Miss Sparks?" asked young Mr Plush.

I shook my head. The cushion I'd seen as I walked through the house was Mrs Morcom's turban. I tried not to stare, and then something odd happened. My fingertips began to tingle again. It felt like the blood was fizzing underneath my skin.

"Your pipe, sir," I whispered, turning to Mr Plush senior. "I think I know where it is."

Then I blushed. It seemed so silly. And what if I was wrong?

"Where is it, my dear?"

I pointed.

"Oh, botheration, Judith." All of a sudden, Mrs Morcom looked more like a kitten than a pug. A mischievous kitten. In a deep, throaty giggle, she said, "We've been caught."

Then they all started talking at once.

"Why is Father's pipe under your hat, Aunt Almeria?"

"I was trying to persuade her to give it back, Papa."

"You are poisoning your body, which as you know, Saddy, is a sacred temple – or should be – with that disgusting tobacco. It was for your own good."

"But it's *healthful*, Almeria. Good for the lungs."

"Pish! Tosh! Poppycock!"

"But why is it under your *hat*?"

And then suddenly they fell silent.

"She found it, Father," said young Mr Plush quietly. "Miss Sparks found it."

"By Jove, she did. She really did." Mr Plush senior put his hand on my shoulder. "Miss Sparks, I think you may be a *teleagtivist*."

Was that someone who lit fires? Or threw bombs? Cook had read to us all about them from the newspaper, I was sure. I stood up. "No, I ain't!"

"A teleagtivist," said young Mr Plush, "is someone who is able to see objects from a distance and find them. It's a term of my father's own devising."

I sat back down. "A tele-what?"

"The *tele* part comes from the Classical Greek language, and means something far off," said Mr Plush senior. "And *ago*; I bring, and finally *visio*; I see. Teleagtivist, you see."

I didn't.

"Miss Sparks, I think you are one of those rare people who can see a thing that is hidden. There are

59

many authenticated instances of telekinesis — which is the act of moving objects by mental effort – but not many of *finding* objects. I have met only one, a most remarkable case, a young sailor from the Hebridean island of Eigg. His fingers, also, itched."

"How tedious you are, Saddy, with your psychic poppycock," interrupted Mrs Morcom. She then said, in a gentler tone, "Saddy, you really mustn't tire Miss Sparks. Remember the poor girl's just fainted."

I looked gratefully at Mrs Morcom. I *was* tired. After all, in the past few days I'd been framed and then sacked; I'd been attacked and rescued; and I'd found out that not only was I adopted, I was also a telega … whatever it was.

But Mr Plush senior ignored his sister.

"I speculate that perhaps when someone is deeply, passionately anxious to find something that is missing, that desire will transfer itself to the teleagtivist, so that—"

"Saddy!" Mrs Morcom rapped him on the shoulder with a rolled newspaper, but he still ignored her.

"So that without a conscious search, the object is found. You did it all the time at Madame Louisette's." He turned to me and smiled. "And here, you've found my favourite pipe." As I said before, he had a lovely smile.

"Judith, rescue her," said Mrs Morcom, and threw her turban at her brother.

"Rescue her?" He looked quite puzzled. "Why does she need to be rescued?"

"Would you like to rest, dear?" asked Miss Plush.

"Yes please, miss." So she took me up to my room, and the rest of the day passed in a dream, sitting in an armchair by a cosy fire and having supper on a tray, and ended in the softest, warmest bed this side of heaven. I went to sleep without a worry in the world about evil designs.

The next morning Etty said, quite casual, that I was to come down to breakfast with the family.

I couldn't work it out. Ladies and gentlemen don't usually have much to do with the likes of me. Servants and shopgirls and apprentices were on one side of the fence, and they were on the other. Still, my whole world had already been turned topsy-turvy. What was one more thing?

Mrs Morcom had breakfast in her room, and Miss Judith only ate eggs and toast, but both Mr Plushes ate ham and kidneys and sausages and fish all full of whiskery bones, as well as the eggs and toast. Amy, a late riser like her mistress, joined us in time for scraps and a dish of milky tea. They all drank a lot of tea, and then read their newspapers (even Miss Judith) and their letters. There was a pile of letters, and though Miss Judith said gently, "Oh, Papa," Mr Plush senior opened them all with his eggy knife.

"Aha!" he said, leaving one large envelope intact and waving it around.

"What is it, Father?" asked young Mr Plush.

"It's our invoice to Lady Throttle, SP. It's got 'Return to sender' written on it. Very quick off the mark, isn't she?"

Perhaps it wasn't my business. But perhaps it was, considering as how it involved Lady Throttle. "Invoice, sir?" I asked. "Is that like the bill, sir?"

"Indeed it is, Miss Sparks." He put it back in the pile. "Perhaps, my dear, you could address me as 'Professor'? You know, I really do prefer it." He beamed his beautiful smile at me. "We are a very informal household. No need for 'Miss Plush', is there?"

Miss Plush – I mean, Judith – smiled and shook her head. "You could also call Saddington here SP, as we all do. It's a lot shorter."

I looked from one to the other. An informal household, he called it. Bloomin' mad, I called it. "Professor" was all right, for it sounded respectful, but how could I – Verity Sparks – address a lady and gentleman as "Judith" and "SP"?

Brother and sister smiled encouragingly.

"Please do," said young Mr Plush.

Orders is orders after all, I thought. "You'd better call me Verity, then, SP, sir," I said. For some reason, they all laughed.

"Professor, sir, was Lady Throttle going to pay you to find the diamond?" I persisted.

"She was."

"And now you've lost money on that job?"

"Yes," said the Professor, seeming quite uncon-cerned. "I suppose we have." Just then the door opened and Etty came in.

"Mr Opie is here, sir," she said. "He says he's sorry to make such an early call, but he has something important to tell you."

I pricked up my ears. Opie? Wasn't it a Mr Opie who'd helped SP to rescue me?

"Ask him to come in right away, please, Etty," said the Professor. "Important information. So soon. Splendid."

The Professor sat back, all smiles, to wait for his visitor, but Judith had gone rather red in the face. She pushed back her chair suddenly and got to her feet.

"Excuse me," she said, so quiet it was almost a

whisper, and left the room. I wondered if perhaps she'd been took ill, but if either gentleman even noticed, they didn't seem concerned. A couple of seconds later, in walked the handsomest young man I'd ever clapped eyes on. He wasn't as tall as SP, but more strongly built, and he had beautiful dark wavy hair, a lovely moustache, bright blue eyes and lashes as thick as silk fringe.

"My dear fellow!" said the Professor, jumping up. "What news?" But SP had better manners and took the trouble to introduce me.

"My dear Miss Sparks. I'm very glad to see you looking so well after your terrible experience of yesterday," said Mr Opie. He stepped forward and shook my hand. "I'm only glad I was able to be of service to you." He gave me a smile like he meant every word, and I felt like a little princess.

"What's more," he said, turning to the Professor, "I was able to find out the scoundrel's identity. His name is Pinner. He's a dog thief by trade."

"A dog thief," said SP. "Can that really be a speciality in crime?"

"Yes," I broke in. I knew about dog stealing. "Any number of our ladies has had their lapdogs taken and a ransom note sent. Five pounds, Lady Purslane paid up, and they didn't even send Pansy back."

"Miss Sparks is right," said Mr Opie. "Valuable dogs are ransomed or even exported, and the cheaper ones are sold for their skins. Dog stealers are very odd fellows; it seems they're bred to that particular kind of crime, and that's why it's highly unusual for this Pinner to have attacked someone."

"Her purse was taken, so it may have been a simple street robbery, even if Pinner was acting out of character," said SP.

"Indeed," said the Professor. "But I wonder why? Why this particular young girl? It's not as if Verity looks particularly prosperous. She wore no jewellery, her clothes were perfectly ordinary and her bag, if she'll forgive me for saying so, was distinctly shabby. Verity, my dear, do you remember anything about the attack? Can you describe what happened?"

I described. I described so much that SP had to scribble to catch up with me, and the Professor shook his head in amazement. "Verity," he said. "Do you know that you have a most remarkable memory?"

"No, sir."

"But you do. You seem to have almost total recall."

"He means that you remember everything," said SP.

"Oh." I'd never thought about it before.

The Professor and SP exchanged a glance, and

then the Professor continued with his questions. "Anything else?"

It was the one thing that really puzzled me about the whole thing. "When I walked past the laneway, the girl called out my name."

"Your name?" the Professor boomed. "She knew your name?"

"Why, yes, sir. She must of, sir."

"D'you hear that, SP? *She knew her name*. Verity, are you sure you've never heard of this Pinner fellow? What's his first name, Opie?"

"Mic-Mac."

"Mic-Mac?" I said. "Why, that's Miss Charlotte's sweetheart."

Over the next few days, it all fell into place. After a few of what the Professor called "discreet inquiries", they found out that Lady Throttle was up to her ears in debt. Too many hats, too many card games and too much keeping up with rich friends. So she hatched a plan to fake the robbery of the Throttle diamond and sell it, thus paying her debts, with her husband none the wiser. Lady Throttle, it turned out, had once been a hat-shop *vendeuse* herself, and that was how she knew Miss Charlotte. Miss Charlotte was in on the scheme, and she'd asked Mic-Mac to retrieve the ruby when my itchy fingers spoiled their plans. It turned out she'd been in on the dog-nappings too.

Anyway, the long and short of it was that the Plushes invited me to continue as their guest until the Throttle affair was all sorted out.

A week later found us with a private appointment at the Throttles'.

Lady Throttle ignored me, but greeted the gents with a charming giggle. I could tell she was nervous. Her little white hands were trembling as she unwrapped a chocolate. "Would you like tea? I'll ring for Crewel."

"No, thank you, Lady Throttle. This is not a social call. It's a business matter."

"I can't think what you mean. Surely our business is concluded. My maid put the wretched thing in my purse. It was found and that's the end of the matter."

"But what of Miss Sparks?"

"Miss Sparks? Who is Miss Sparks? I've never heard of her."

"Miss Sparks is here in the room with us, Lady Throttle."

She reddened slightly. "The girl, you mean."

"Yes, the girl. This girl. You were quite happy for this girl to be tried and found guilty of theft. You were quite happy for her to go to prison. And when your plot failed, you took your spiteful revenge. You had her dismissed from her place. Do you know what that can mean for a young girl in a city like London? Do you, Lady Throttle?" The Professor's voice got louder and louder. He rose to his feet, looking very tall and stern, a bit like a hellfire preacher I once saw in the street, only better dressed.

"It's ... it's nothing to do with me," she said faintly.

"I think it is."

"Not at all," she said, rallying. "I shall tell all my friends. I have many friends, Mr Plush, and you'd better believe it. Rest assured you and your son will never find any clients again. Lady Archcape was the one who recommended you to me. Just wait until I tell her."

"Just wait until I tell your husband," said the Professor.

Her rosebud mouth fell open and her eyes bulged slightly. The chocolate box fell to the floor. "What do you want?"

"I want our fee, I want you to pay your bill to Madame Louisette's, and I want Miss Sparks, should she so choose, to be reinstated in her place of employment."

"That's ... that's blackmail."

"No. That's justice, Lady Throttle."

"But I haven't got any money," she wailed.

"Economise, my dear lady."

"Economise." She said the word so savagely she almost spat. "I know all about economising. Growing up in mended gowns and retrimmed hats and always moving to cheaper lodgings and grimier streets."

"Save the tragic tale for a sympathetic audience," interrupted the Professor. "We will accept our fee in instalments, and I am sure Madame Louisette would be happy if you commence paying your account."

Her beautiful face was now all crumpled up and red. "You won't ... you won't tell..."

"Our service is completely confidential, Lady Throttle," said the Professor, bowing, and the three of us left the room.

"It'll be funny being back at Madame's after this," I said as we walked to the waiting carriage.

"Back at Madame's? Whatever do you mean?" said the Professor.

"Just what you said back there at Lady Throttle's. She's going to talk to Madame and restate me, or something. So I can go back to work there. Isn't that what you meant?"

"Yes and no," said the Professor. "Naturally, I want Lady Throttle to withdraw her threats to your former employer. But, my dear young friend, I think you could be of inestimable value to us in our investigatory endeavours."

I must have looked blank again (it happened dozens of times a day at the start, until I got myself a vocabulary) and SP rephrased his father's words so I could understand.

"We need you, Verity. We've got a new case, and we think you can help us solve it. Won't you please stay with us a little while longer?"

"Your amazing memory, not to mention your, ah, *itchy* fingers, would make you a most valuable assistant. And we really do need a female operative. A sharp-eyed young girl would make all the difference to some of our inquiries," said the Professor. "We would provide you with accommodation and a wage of ... let me see ... how does twenty pounds a year sound? With a dress allowance. Would that suit? Unless, of course, you wish to return to Madame Louisette's. Do you?"

I thought about the cold early mornings. The omnibus drivers who wouldn't stop and the snooty clients and the stuffy workroom. The pricked fingers and the eyestrain.

"No," I said. "I'll stay."

❖ ❖ ❖

At Madame Louisette's we used to line bonnets with a material called shot silk. Depending on how you looked at it, it was purple or green, and if you held it just right you'd see the two colours together. I felt just like that – first one thing, then another, and sometimes all of a mixture – and although that night after supper I went to my bedroom feeling excited and happy, before I knew it I was crying. I wasn't much of a one for crying, as a rule. Living with Uncle Bill and Auntie Sarah had knocked it out of me, for you were just as likely to get a hiding as a hug in that household. Tears never fixed anything, anyway. But I couldn't help it.

"You stop that, Verity Sparks," I scolded myself. "You are a very lucky girl."

I had kind friends, and a job, and a home. But Mulberry Hill wasn't home. Then, neither was Madame Louisette's. Or – I shuddered – Uncle Bill and Auntie Sarah's stinking rats' nest in Racketty Lane. My real home was with Ma and Pa, and it was lost to me for ever when they died. Tonight I missed them so much it hurt. I didn't care if they weren't my real mother and father; they were the only parents I'd ever known, and you could never hope to meet a kinder, more loving couple. My eyes filled up with tears again.

All of a sudden I remembered Ma's things. I kneeled on the floor, felt around in my carpetbag and brought out a patched old petticoat. I'd bundled them up inside it, in case of prying fingers at Madame Louisette's. I took them out one by one.

First, the ring. It was made of three intertwined bands, each of a different metal. I knew it wasn't Ma's wedding ring – that got sold when Uncle Bill and Auntie Sarah took me in – and I couldn't recall ever seeing Ma wear it. Still, she'd saved it and kept it for me, and that made it precious. It was a bit too big, but I slipped it on my finger just the same.

I held up the quilt next. It was the size of a baby blanket, made of triangles pieced together to form stars. The sewing of it was perfection, every tiny stitch even and neat. Where did Ma get such fancy material? I knew from Madame's what fine French silks like these could cost. Another mystery.

Last, the coin; the lucky piece, Ma called it. It was thin and battered, with a hole drilled in the top, hung on a length of red silk cord. It must be foreign money, I thought, turning it over. Or maybe not even money at all. Perhaps it was a medal of some kind. One side had the letter "V" on it, very faint, as if half rubbed off, and the other had seven little stars making a lopsided cross set inside a circle.

I put the quilt on the bed, tucked the ring under my pillow and slipped the lucky piece on its cord over my head. The ring, the lucky piece and the quilt — my three gifts from Ma. I closed my eyes and pictured her face, not flushed with the fever as I last saw her, but smiling, like she used to. I knew Ma would be glad I was here, with a job and with friends. Feeling comforted at last, I snuggled down in the bed and fell asleep.

6

THE CASE OF THE CHINA HORSE

I slept like a log and woke up feeling cheerful, even excited. Today I'd begin my very first investigation.

"Now, my dears," said the Professor over breakfast. "Let me give you some background information."

"The case concerns a Chinese horse, doesn't it?" asked Judith.

"Indeed. A very valuable horse."

"A racehorse?" I asked.

"No, a figurine. That's like a little statue," said the Professor. He didn't laugh at me for my ignorance, and neither did Judith. "It's an antiquity." He went on to explain that an antiquity is something very, very old. This one was a figure of a horse made in China over a thousand years ago.

"Our client, Mrs Honeychurch, contacted the Confidential Inquiry Agency in great distress," said the Professor. "She is a widow, about sixty, childless, quite rich, and living quietly with a couple of maids and a housekeeper. Her pride and joy is a collection of Oriental antiquities, acquired with her late husband when they lived in Canton."

"Does she know for certain sure that this little horse has been nicked?" I asked. "It could just have been broken by one of the maids while she was dusting."

"We are almost certain it has been taken. It is a very delicate matter," the Professor told us. "The lady suspects an old friend. His name is Major Wilton. He too collects Chinese antiquities. Now, it seems that a month ago, Mrs Honeychurch observed the Major slipping a valuable decorated bowl into his pocket. She didn't know what to do or say, she told me, but the bowl was back in its place the next day. She is quite wretched now, for she wonders whether temptation has got the better of him."

"How terrible," said Judith.

"She has invited him to visit her today. And Verity, you and Judith and I are to be guests as well. For afternoon tea."

Afternoon tea? I looked down at my shabby dress, and Judith caught my eye. Read my mind too.

"If you come upstairs with me later," she whispered, "I will find one of my old dresses that will fit you. Mrs Cannister can help us take up the hem."

I blushed and thanked her. Maybe a smart dress wouldn't help to find whoever nobbled the antiquities, but it'd make me feel a lot better at this tea party.

Mrs Honeychurch lived in Gordon Square, in a terrace set behind a quiet tree-shaded park. As the Professor helped Judith and then me out of the carriage, a child darted out from the servant's entrance and up to the horses. It was a little boy of about five, with wide-apart blue eyes, an elfin face and a shock of white-blond hair.

"Jimmy! Jimmy!" A lady came running out of the house. "I'm sorry," she said, taking his hand. "He's mad on horses, and I can't keep him away from them. Why, only last week he followed a delivery cart all the way up the Euston Road."

"It's no bother to me," said John, the Plushes' coachman. "You can pat 'em, sonny. Go on."

"All right then, Jimmy," the lady said and she turned to us, still a bit flustered over her runaway. I thought it was Mrs Honeychurch herself, for she was dressed very nicely, but it turned out it was only the housekeeper. Mrs Chalmers was her name, and she led us into the hall and down a corridor to the drawing room.

"Mrs Honeychurch is expecting you," she said, ushering us in.

Light filtered in through the narrow curtained windows, and it was all dim and solemn, like a church. The walls were lined with shelves and glass cases full of china bowls and plates. Some were painted with flowers and insects and strange winged creatures; some were patterned with blue and white; some were quite plain, and one – deep red and shiny and shaped like an upturned tulip – was so beautiful it took my breath away.

"I see you are looking at the *sang-de-boeuf*," said a woman's voice.

"Oh," I said, startled. A little lady, old but still lovely in a thistledown sort of way, was sitting on the sofa.

"*Sang-de-boeuf* means oxblood," she went on. "It's from the Ming Dynasty."

It was still gobbledegook to me, but the Professor was impressed.

"Amazing," he said. "We must beg your pardon, Mrs Honeychurch. I can speak for all of us. Your collection has deprived us, momentarily, of speech."

"Thank you," said Mrs Honeychurch, holding out her hand.

The Professor, with another of his old-fashioned

bows, kissed it, and then did the introductions. "Our young friend, Miss Sparks," was the way he put it when he came to me, and he never said a thing about the millinery trade.

"It is certainly a wonderful collection, Mrs Honeychurch," said the Professor. "The work of many years, I can tell. Could you perhaps show me the bowl that Major Wilton…"

The Professor trailed off tactfully, but I could see the lady was upset. She dabbed her eyes with her hankie, and sighed, and then sighed again, more deeply, and pointed to a small pink bowl decorated with fruit, vines and flowers.

"My favourite. Qing Dynasty. Pretty, isn't it? And my husband's favourite was the Tang horse. It is very valuable, but Mr Honeychurch loved it because the conformation of the rump and the hocks reminded him of his old hunter Mazeppa." A tiny tear trickled down her cheek.

There was a knock on the door.

"The Major," announced Mrs Chalmers.

Major Wilton was short and round and red in the face, a tubby whirlwind of waving hands, wobbling chins, nods and beaming smiles.

"Dear Lydia!" he boomed. "How charming you look. Are you well? A little low? Let's see if I can't cheer you up." Only then did he notice the Professor, Judith and me. "And visitors? What a treat. Young ladies too." He bowed over our hands, beaming all the while. "How delightful."

A maid came in with the tea tray, and the Major jumped up and down like a jack-in-the-box: passing the cups, offering milk or sugar or lemon, handing around the cucumber sandwiches, urging Mrs Honeychurch, Judith and me to have one of the pretty iced cakes.

"I know how partial you ladies are to sweets," he said. He gazed adoringly at our hostess. "Sweets to the sweet, eh?"

I felt like laughing. The Major steal the horse? He'd have given Mrs Honeychurch the shirt off his back. It was plain as the nose on your face that he simply worshipped her. Besides, I already knew where the horse was. My fingers had started to itch.

I wasn't sure what to do next.

"Professor," I whispered, plucking at his coat sleeve, but he wasn't paying attention, for Major Wilton had bobbed to his feet.

"I nearly forgot," he cried. "I have something for you, dear Lydia. A surprise. I left it with Mrs Chalmers. I'll just go and fetch it."

"You see?" said Mrs Honeychurch after he had

left the room. "I'm sure he has something on his conscience."

"Professor…" I tried again, but the Major bounced back into the room carrying a large brown-paper parcel. He placed it gently on Mrs Honeychurch's lap.

"Won't you unwrap it, Lydia? Here, let me help you."

He cut the string with his pocket knife. Inside the brown paper was tissue paper, and inside the tissue was something pink. He shook it out and held it up for her. It was a shawl, embroidered all over with wandering vines, leaves and fruits, flowers and butterflies.

"Oh, Robert. It is the exact pattern of my Qing bowl."

"It is!" crowed the Major. "I had it made for you, Lydia. Do you like it?"

"It's perfect." She stood up and took the Major's hand in hers. "Robert, so that is why you took the Qing bowl."

He looked self-conscious. "Caught me out, did you? Well, I confess I did, Lydia, but only so the embroideress could draw out the design. I put it back the next day."

"You have not also borrowed the Tang horse, Major?" asked the Professor.

"Goodness no. Whatever gave you that idea? Lydia?" He turned to her. "What is this all about?"

"I thought ... your collection ... the horse ... the temptation..."

The Major sat down heavily. "So this is what you think of me. My dear, I began my collection so that you and I would have something in common. I'd have collected live snakes if you'd liked them." He mopped his face with his handkerchief. "My dear," he said, taking her hand. "I would not make you unhappy for all the tea in China."

This was my chance. "I think I know where it is," I said.

All the eyes in the room were on me, and suddenly I felt shy.

"Mrs Honeychurch, may I try to find it?"

"Of course, dear. Go wherever you like," said Mrs Honeychurch, but really, she didn't give two hoots for the china horse now. She was gazing at Major Wilton with stars in her eyes.

I slipped out of the room, with the Professor behind me, and nearly ran smack-bang into Mrs Chalmers.

"Mrs Chalmers," I said. "May we see Jimmy's room?"

"Well..." She stopped, looking worried. "I suppose so."

I was off before she'd finished, up one flight of stairs and then the next. On the top landing I paused. My fingers were itching and I could see that little horse clear as day. A beautiful horse he was, already saddled, standing poised and graceful with one hoof raised, waiting for his rider.

"Wait, Miss Sparks!" It was Mrs Chalmers, puffing, followed by the Professor. "That one is Jimmy's room." Her face was white. "I've already searched," she whispered. "Even in the bed."

"Is James your grandson, Mrs Chalmers?" asked the Professor. He spoke very gently.

"Yes, sir. My daughter's boy. She died of the cholera last summer."

I rubbed my hands together, wincing a bit, for by now my fingers felt just like I had chilblains. I couldn't see the little horse any more; I could see bars. Perhaps Jimmy's room had once been meant for a nursery and there were bars on the windows.

Mrs Chalmers opened the door. "Have a look, if you want."

The bars weren't on the windows but on the cot. My fingers stopped itching. I kneeled at the end of James's cot, lifted a loose floorboard and there was the Tang horse in a bed of straw. I held it up into the light. He had been well stabled. There was not a chip or a crack on him.

"Oh, dear," said Mrs Chalmers. "I asked him and he said no. He's never told me lies before." Tears welled in her eyes, but she brushed them away and said in a business-like tone, "Well, thank goodness it's found. But Miss, how did you know?"

"I saw how mad on horses he was. And I used to hide my treasures," I said. "There was a loose floorboard under my bed too." Even though it wasn't the whole story, it was quite true.

I handed the horse over to the Professor, for now that my hands weren't itching, they felt so weak that I was scared I'd drop the blessed thing. We trooped down the stairs and into the drawing room, and Mrs Chalmers went outside to get Jimmy. He came in, clinging to his grandmother's skirts, but when Mrs Honeychurch asked him if he knew where the missing Tang horse might be, he shook his head.

"Don't know no Tang," he whispered.

"Then what's this?" asked Mrs Chalmers, pointing to the china horse in the Professor's hands. She was close to either tears or temper, I could tell, but her face changed when the little boy spoke.

"That's Mazeppa," he said, surprised. "No one asked me 'bout Mazeppa."

"Jimmy," she said sorrowfully, but Mrs Honeychurch began to laugh.

"You know that it was very wrong of you, don't you, James, to put Mazeppa in your stable without asking?" said Mrs Honeychurch. "Everyone was so worried about him. Please put him back."

"Yes, ma'am," whispered James. He took the horse from the Professor and placed it carefully on the shelf. "Lovely, he is." He stroked its shiny brown back. "Lovely."

Mrs Honeychurch sat a few seconds, thinking. "James," she said. "You may have him."

Jimmy stared at her.

"He's yours."

"What do you say, Jimmy?" prompted Mrs Chalmers.

Jimmy stammered out his thanks, but Mrs Honeychurch wasn't listening. The Major had hold of her hand, and she was staring into his eyes like he was Romeo and Prince Charming all in one. We tiptoed away.

"It just goes to show," said the Professor to Judith and me when we were back in the carriage.

"What, Father?"

"There is such a thing as a happy ending." He dabbed at his eyes with his handkerchief, and then blew his nose very hard. "Touch of hay fever," he explained, then turned to me. "Well done, Verity. Perhaps we should add matchmaking to our prospectus."

7

A MEETING OF THE SIPP

When I look back at all the things I learned in those first few months as an Assistant Confidential Inquiry Agent, it's a wonder my brain didn't burst.

First, there was Surveillance. That meant following people and watching what they did.

"Remember, any small detail might be the vital clue we need to crack the case," said SP.

And then I had to learn Reporting.

"Father says you have remarkable powers of observation – that means noticing things, Verity – and at times you must take notes about what you've seen." SP hesitated, as if he was embarrassed. "Do you ... er ... can you read and write?"

I wasn't too offended. Lots of girls like me couldn't, but I was lucky; Ma had taught me my letters when I was small. Even so, I was a bit rusty, and SP took on the job of bringing me up to scratch.

We started with the *London Illustrated Journal* and soon I was picking and choosing from the Professor's library. Who would have thought of a milliner's apprentice reading Mr William Shakespeare and Miss Jane Austen?

Judith's job was Manners and Deportment. I had to be able to go with her to a concert or a tea party or a smart shop without giving the game away that I was in fact a Female Operative. I was nearly over saying "ain't" and dropping my aitches, and Judith was pleased. I was easy to teach, she said, for my voice was sweet and low, and I was naturally quite refined.

"Ha!" said Mrs Morcom. "I've heard refined young ladies that shriek like cockatoos. You are an excellent teacher though, Judith. Verity is not exactly a sow's ear, but I do believe she will be a silk purse by the time you have done with her."

It was book-learning with SP and tea parties with Judith, but with the Professor it was all Experiments.

"Experiment" was a new word to me, but I learned its meaning only too well. So well that my heart sank to my boots every time I heard the Professor say it. At first it was fun, but after a while a few hours trimming hats would have seemed like a holiday to me.

This is what we did. I'd be blindfolded, and the Professor and I would sit either side of a table, with a screen between us. He'd shuffle a pack of cards and then place one of them on his side and ask me to guess what it was. And what do you know? Right from the first, I hardly ever got one wrong. That got the Professor very excited. After the playing cards, we moved on to coloured shapes and wooden animals and words written on pieces of card. All these childish games were highly interesting to the Professor, but to me they were strange and a bit scary. It was sort of like finding you can speak French or play the piano, just like that, with never a lesson or a teacher. I found myself trying to ignore the itchy fingers, trying not to see the pictures in my head. But the Professor was unstoppable.

"Excellent, excellent," he'd say, and write it all up in his big leather-bound book. He put in the time and date and how long it took for me to guess, and my answers to his questions. Well, question, really. He said it different ways, but it was always the same one.

"How do you do it?"

I couldn't tell him. I wanted to, but I couldn't. I just didn't know.

"These experiments, sir," I said one morning. "Can I ask you what they are for?"

The Professor stroked his moustache, and thought a little. "In this modern scientific age," he began, "we have to assume that there are in fact real explanations for events and occurrences that in the past were seen as pure mysteries." He smiled his beautiful smile and patted my shoulder. "As a very great man, a friend of mine, said, 'Every fact is a theory, if we did but know it.' And so my aim is to gather as many facts about your gift as possible, so that my fellow researchers and I can put them under the light of scientific analysis."

"Fellow searchers?"

"Ah, my dear child. You've said it." He looked at me very kindly and fondly. "We are indeed searchers: searchers after truth in dark and hidden places. We call ourselves the Society for the Investigation of Psychic Phenomena. A small group as yet, but some fine minds. In fact, there is a meeting here tonight. I would like it very much if you would join us."

"So you can show me off, Professor?"

The Professor choked on his tea, and I wondered if I'd been rude.

"No, Verity. Well, actually, yes. But not if you truly dislike the idea."

I did. I could just see it: a pack of toffs all looking on while I did tricks like an organ-grinder's monkey.

But I didn't have the heart to say no. The Professor was so excited about his notes and his experiments, and who was I to spoil his fun?

"I would like to do something a little different too. I will describe the way you found the brooch and my pipe and the horse, but I would also like you, if you would, to demonstrate the finding of a hidden item," he said.

"Yes?" I said, trying hard to sound willing.

"It would be a splendid addition to our data." He rubbed his hands together. "I will ask one or two of our members to secrete some small objects in the room before you come in, while another pair keeps watch in the passageway, to make sure you are not peeping through the keyhole. And Verity, could you put your mind to the toasting fork?"

"The toasting fork?" Whatever next! Sometimes the Professor's mind leapt about like a barrel of monkeys.

"It's been missing since last week."

They came at eight, and after half an hour of official SIPP business, the Professor came and got me. There were seven members of the SIPP gathered in the library, but I was too nervous to notice much more than a varied collection of beards and moustaches, some very dreary dresses on the ladies, and even drearier bonnets.

"My fellow searchers," the Professor began. "I would like to introduce Miss Verity Sparks. Miss Sparks has kindly consented to be with us tonight, to demonstrate her skills as a teleagtivist." There was some whispered comment, and the Professor went on. "Teleagtivism, as you all know, is a word of my own devising; some of you of course will prefer the catch-all 'telepathy', but we may leave that issue for another meeting. I would like to assure you all that Miss Sparks is not a professional, has never mounted the stage and has never given any exhibition or display. Miss Sparks, may I present Sir Maximilian Orffe, Mrs Rose, Professors Choate and Flange, Mr Savinov, Miss Kelling and our newest member, Doctor Beale."

We did the usual. I named the cards and I found the small objects, including the toasting fork that the Professor had really and truly mislaid. (It was in the coal scuttle.) But we didn't go on too long; I think Mrs Morcom must have had a quiet talk to the Professor about performing dogs and the like, and it was all rather well-mannered and respectful, with a lot of "If you please, Miss Sparks" and "Thank you, Miss Sparks". At the end, he asked me if I would be prepared to answer one or two questions from the meeting.

Doctor Beale stood up. He had narrow shoulders but a very big head, and thin mousy hair slicked back with oil. He was clean-shaven, which was unusual; most gentlemen preferred beards and moustaches, and a few whiskers would have balanced out his large, white forehead. The room was too dim for me to judge the colour of his eyes, but they were pale, and when he fixed them on me I couldn't help giving a little shiver, as if I'd stepped out into the cold. All in all, he was rather odd, but I don't think that was why I took an instant dislike to him.

"Miss Sparks," he said, speaking very slowly and precisely, as if each word was snipped off with scissors. "Can you tell me if any other member of your family exhibited special gifts?"

"No, sir," I said. My family tree – or lack of – was none of his business.

"And have you ever taken part in any programme of experimentation before?"

"No, sir."

"Aha. In your opinion, Miss Sparks, how are the experiments impacting upon your abilities? Have you noticed an increase, or indeed a diminishing of your powers?"

"Beg pardon, sir?"

"He's asking if you are getting better or worse,"

said Mrs Rose in a loud whisper.

"Nothing much has changed, sir," I said.

That wasn't exactly true. I knew that all the practising was making me better at it, but I met the Professor's eyes and he gave a tiny little nod, as if agreeing with my short answers. I got the impression that he didn't like Dr Beale very much.

Then Miss Kelling wanted to know if I visualised in black-and-white, and Mrs Rose wondered if I felt tired afterwards, and I said no to that one and yes to the other, and then asked to be excused.

"Miss Sparks, permit me to detain you for a minute longer," said a deep fruity voice. It was Mr Savinov. He'd been sitting quietly at the back of the room, but as he rose I saw that he was a fine-looking old man, tall and so burly he was almost bursting out of his evening suit. His hair was long and brushed back from his face in thick silver-grey waves, and his beard and moustache were neatly trimmed. His calm, stern face reminded me of the bronze lions in Trafalgar Square.

"Miss Sparks, your skills are remarkable, and so is your patience. I would like to thank you on behalf of all of us —" he gestured to those gathered in the library — "and to wish you well."

There was a polite round of applause, and I think

I blushed red as a beetroot. Fancy that, I thought. Compliments to Verity Sparks. I looked back into the room just as I was closing the door, and Mr Savinov caught my eye. He gave me a little smile, as if we two were in on the same secret. I smiled back. I was still smiling when I got upstairs to my room.

I wasn't smiling twenty minutes later. The Professor sent Etty to ask if I'd come to his study for a moment.

"The doctor's there with him," she told me.

"Dr Beale?"

"That's the one," said Etty, making a face. So she didn't like him either.

I let myself in and shut the door. The two men were standing side by side in front of the fire, and in spite of the warmth, there was a frosty kind of feeling in the room.

"Dr Beale has something to ask you, Verity," said the Professor. His voice sounded very strange. I wondered what was the matter with him. "Go on, Doctor."

He got straight to the point. "Miss Sparks, I want to request your valuable assistance in a vital matter of scientific research." He paused, looking at me. Close up, his eyes were pale green and reminded me of fishes' eyes, and his skin had an odd, waxy sheen to it. "No more than one week's investigation would be involved, and I am prepared to pay you fifty pounds for your co-operation." It was clear he expected I'd jump at the chance to make fifty pounds – after all, it was a small fortune – and he stretched his mouth open in what I suppose he thought was a smile. "What do you say, Miss Sparks?"

I didn't want to help Dr Beale in anything, no matter how vital. He gave me the creeps. "I'm already doing experiments with the Professor," I said.

Dr Beale raised his eyebrows. "I have advised Professor Plush that to wilfully stand in the way of progress for purely personal reasons is selfishness of the highest order, and will reap its own punishment. Neither should he stand in the way of letting you better yourself by receiving a considerable financial reward, which would allow you to become independent of your so-called benefactors and friends."

"So-called?" I didn't like the sneer in Dr Beale's voice. "I'm not sure what benefactors are, but I know my friends when I see them."

"So you may think." Dr Beale smirked. "You are, if you will forgive my analogy, the goose that lays the golden eggs, and so of course Professor Plush is kind to you. Sheer self-interest."

The Professor made an odd little noise in his

throat, but said not one word. I wanted to say something very rude, for who was Dr Beale to call me a goose? But I kept silent too. Acting like that is called dignity, Judith taught me.

"My sister, Miss Anna Beale, will be pleased to receive you and of course act as chaperone," Dr Beale continued. "What do you say, Miss Sparks?"

"I don't want to," I said flatly.

Our eyes met. The way he looked at me, I could have been an insect. An interesting insect, one that he wanted to catch and put in a jar and investigate. But not a person. Not me, Verity Sparks. He was silent for a few seconds, and then his face gave a kind of twitch.

"Miss Sparks," he said, bowing slightly, and then he turned to the Professor. "Well, sir," he said. "The young lady has spoken, and I have failed in my quest. I have no hard feelings, I assure you, Miss Sparks. I bid you both good night."

We heard the front door slam a few seconds later.

"That man!" shouted the Professor. "That ... that man."

Now I knew what had been wrong with his voice. He'd wanted to yell.

He paced up and down for a few seconds and then snatched a vase from the mantelpiece and deliberately threw it onto the hearth. "There," he said, looking at the smashed pieces. "That feels better. Now find me the bannister brush, Verity, and I'll hide the evidence from Etty."

8

CALLISTEMON CITRINUS

"I hear you had a flattering offer last night," said SP after breakfast the next morning.

"Do tell, Verity," said Judith, but when I did she made a face. "How odd."

"He hasn't the best reputation, has he?" said SP.

"The man's a pest!" exploded the Professor.

"What has he done?" asked Judith.

The Professor calmed down, then said with a sigh, "Apparently, he's up to the last chapters of his book. He's convinced it's going to make the whole world sit up and take notice, but he needs another subject for his experiments now Madame Oblomov has taken her son back to Moscow. Beale thought Verity here would fit the bill perfectly. Offered to pay her. Sister will chaperone, and all that. But I could never have allowed Verity to accept his offer, even if she'd been tempted. I believe that Dr Beale has performed some most irregular experiments."

"What sort?" I asked.

"It is said that he obtained a number of children from an orphanage. He wanted to find out whether certain fears are innate or acquired." He hesitated. "Rumour is that one of the children died."

"How dreadful," said Judith.

"What happened to the other children?" I asked.

"They went back to the orphanage, I suppose. It was hushed up, of course, and there were some who thought nothing of it." He gave a little grunt. "I must say I wish the man hadn't joined our little group. But there was a letter of introduction from Professor James of Harvard, you see, and I couldn't really say no."

"Verity, you don't have to see him again," said SP. "Does she, Father?"

"Certainly not. In fact, when I agreed to let him talk to you last night, Verity, it was on the condition that if you refused, he was not to communicate with you again." He changed the subject. "And how did you enjoy the gathering last night?"

"It wasn't near as bad as I'd thought it would be," I said honestly. "I did like Mr Savinov."

"Ah!" said the Professor. "Dear Pierre. I am lunching with him at the Megatherium Club today.

He's a fine fellow, and a most interesting man as well. He's done many things. Born in Russia, made his fortune in furs and timber in Canada, and now has businesses all over the Continent."

"Have you known him long?" I asked.

"No, no. I met him only a couple of years ago. He's a good friend of our neighbour, Monsieur Tissot. Have you met Tissot yet, Verity? Judith is thick as thieves with his wife, Kathleen."

I had been to quite a few tea parties with Judith, but not yet to the Tissots. I shook my head, wanting to hear more about Mr Savinov, but all the Professor said was, "Such a tragedy."

Did he mean the Tissots or Mr Savinov? I waited for him to explain himself, but, still eating his toast, he picked up his morning's letters and left the room.

"So, no experiments today?" said SP with a quick grin. He knew how I felt. "Do you want to skip lessons as well?"

"Lessons?" said Judith, standing up and dropping a light kiss on her brother's cheek. "Can't we let the poor child alone? Sometimes I think we're working her much too hard."

Too hard! If only she knew.

"Come on, Verity," said Judith. "Aunt Almeria and I are bored to tears. Please come and talk to us. You come too, SP. I think Antony and Cleopatra are due their breakfast."

I couldn't see Mrs Morcom at first. Or the snakes, and that made me nervous.

"There's nothing to fear, Verity. They're all tucked up in their case," said Judith. "I think Aunt must be at her easel."

The easel turned out to be a wooden stand. Propped onto it was a board, and on the board was a picture. It was a mass of greenery and palm fronds and some kind of fruit, and half-hidden in it was a snake.

"Did you do that, ma'am?"

"I did."

"It looks real."

Mrs Morcom smiled. "I've taken a little artistic licence with the colouring," she said. "But it's generally quite accurate. The palm – *Macrozamia moorei* – is the real subject, of course." She turned to Judith. "Now, where's that brother of yours, Judith? Too busy to see his aunt today?"

"He's gone to get their rats, Aunt."

I was puzzled. "What's the rats for?"

Mrs Morcom raised her eyebrows. They were very thick, whiskery eyebrows, and underneath them her eyes were bright and beady, like those of a small wild creature. She smiled as she said, "To eat."

"Oh."

"What did you think snakes lived on?"

I turned and stared at Antony and Cleopatra, peacefully coiled up in their large glass case. "Grass?"

"Snakes need live meat, Verity. 'Nature, red in tooth and claw,' as Tennyson says. Tennyson," she explained kindly, "is one of our great English poets. Except it's fang and constrictor muscles in this case. Ah, there you are."

SP had returned with a box. Out of it he plucked a large black-and-white rat. It hung there placidly as he held it by the tail with one hand, opened the top of the glass case with the other hand, and quickly dropped it inside. The rat took a few little steps, and sniffed. It sniffed again, nibbled at something on the floor of the case, twitched its whiskers, and nibbled some more, quite unaware of what was uncoiling only a few inches away.

"Don't watch, Verity," said Judith.

I sensed rather than saw Cleopatra's head dart forward, for she moved as quick as lightning. In a trice, she was coiled a couple of times around the rat's body and clamping her jaws around its head.

"You're not going to faint again, are you?" asked Mrs Morcom.

"No, ma'am."

"Sit down then, child. You've gone green."

The next time I glanced her way, Cleopatra had just the rat's rump and long pink tail sticking out of her mouth. It was quite a business, I could see, getting a big fat rat down a snake's gullet. How uncomfortable, I thought.

"It's too big."

"She'll swallow it all right," said SP. "But she's often stuck like that for minutes at a time."

"Ugh." I shuddered a bit. "Poor rat."

"It didn't know what hit it," said Mrs Morcom. "And it wasn't a poor rat at all. It was a very pampered rat, raised with the best of care by Ben O'Brien, the gardener's boy. SP's going to feed Antony now, so turn away, if it bothers you. Would you like to see some more of my paintings? Go into my studio – there, girl, over there. See that portfolio on the desk?"

Mrs Morcom's studio was a little room off the conservatory. In it was a large desk, another easel, and shelves from floor to ceiling, full of books and jars of brushes and tablets of paint and dried plants and shells and tangles of snakeskins and bones and birds' nests and catkins and goodness knows what else. I bet the housemaids cursed when it came to dusting. The portfolio – which was a big cardboard folder – was where she said, on the desk.

"Open it, my dear," she said as I came back out into the conservatory. "You'll like that lot. They're all flowers."

"Mrs Morcom, they're beautiful."

"Of course," she said.

"What's that one, ma'am?" I asked, pointing.

"A waterlily."

"And that one?"

"A magnolia. *Magnolia campbellii*. I painted that in the foothills of the Himalayas, in India. And the waterlily was done in India too."

India! I wondered for a second if Mrs Morcom was a missionary, but somehow she didn't seem the type.

"Aunt is a botanical illustrator," explained Judith. "That was why she was in India. She has travelled all over the world drawing and painting plants."

"She has had several books published," said SP. "And there is a gallery dedicated to her works in Kew Gardens."

That meant nothing much to me until SP explained that all the most famous plant scientists in the world came to study at the Royal Botanical Gardens in Kew.

"Aunt Almeria is a very famous lady," added SP.

"Piffle," she said. "I'd rather be rich than famous,

but I haven't done so badly. After all, it is unusual for a woman to earn her own living as I do."

"Is it?" I said, surprised. "I know lots. Why, there's Madame and Miss Musquash and..." I trailed off. They were all looking at me. Had I said something wrong?

Mrs Morcom was nodding her head. "It is unusual for *ladies*, Verity dear. It seems that the more wealth and respectability a woman has, the less independence she is allowed. I count myself very lucky. Ah, Etty. What is it?"

Etty had a message for SP. "Mr Opie is waiting for you, sir."

"Opie? Capital." SP jumped up. "Thank you, Etty. You'll excuse me, Aunt?"

"Why don't you bring him in here? I like the boy. I'd like to see him again."

Judith made a funny noise in her throat, halfway between a cough and a sob.

"Now, Judith," Mrs Morcom said in a very gentle voice. "Steady, my dear."

"I'll go and see him in the study, Aunt." SP got up to go, but Judith rushed out of the room in front of him. That was the second time she'd left the room rather than meet Mr Opie. Why didn't she like him?

"Oh, dear." Mrs Morcom chewed the end of her paintbrush, turning her lips bright green. "Oh, dear.

That was stupid of me." She looked at me and sighed. "I suppose she has gone to her room and is crying her eyes out."

"Why, ma'am?"

"Why? Because Judith is breaking her heart over Mr Opie, that's why."

"I see," I said. A broken heart. Now Judith's behaviour to Mr Opie made sense.

"Daniel Opie is not only extremely handsome," she said. "He's also extremely nice." She sighed again. "He and Judith are made for each other, but he's got an over-developed sense of honour, the silly boy, and says it can never be. Never is a long, long time, don't you think?"

I couldn't disagree with that.

"Daniel's father was an attorney in some mill town up in the North. He was a bright boy, but there wasn't the money to put him through university. Still, he got a position as an articled clerk with a firm of lawyers in Frogmouth Court. Rumbelow and Budd, they were called. One day young Mr Budd asked Daniel to get a letter from a file. Which he did. Well, it turned out that Mr Budd lost it, there was no copy made, it resulted in the loss of a case, and Mr Budd put the blame on Daniel. He was disgraced, dismissed and, without any money, was soon out on the streets without food or shelter. When SP found him, over a year ago, he was about to jump into the river and end it all."

"SP saved him?"

"Grabbed him by the arm, wrestled him to the ground and talked sense into the young fool. SP recognized him, you see. He and the Professor had done a little work for Rumbelow and Budd, and he'd noticed young Daniel. It was a very lucky thing."

I knew about people jumping in the river. From Cook, of course. If you didn't drown, then you caught typhoid and died anyway.

"Is ... is the Professor against it, then?" I asked.

"No, not really. It's Daniel himself; he declares he isn't fit to black her boots and so on and so forth, like the hero of some rubbishy novel, and so that's why Judith's breaking her heart upstairs. He'll get over it, though," she added confidently.

"Over Judith?"

"No, over the high morals." She chuckled. "High morals are such a bore, dear. Never had much time for them myself." She mixed another splodge of green, and I went back to the portfolio.

I must have been there ten minutes or more. Silk flowers on bonnets was all the botany I knew, so I'd never seen the likes of these. There was one like little velvety claws, and another like a bright red bottlebrush. I peered closer at the paper. How clever Mrs Morcom was. All those dozens and dozens of fine brushstrokes.

Suddenly, my fingers began to itch, and just as suddenly they stopped. But instead of the paper and the bottlebrush flower there was a blinding light, and a thin high piping sound. Something slid past my feet, and then there was blackness, and misery, and the most awful pain in my heart. And I was sitting on the floor, with Mrs Morcom holding a glass to my lips. The water was green from Mrs Morcom's paintbrush, and I shook my head.

"I'm … I'm not sick, ma'am. It's just … when I looked at that picture…"

"You mean this one? The bottlebrush?"

"Yes. I saw … I saw something."

"What?"

"I don't know." Tears began running down my face. I couldn't help it.

"What?" Mrs Morcom shook me. "What?"

"I think it was a snake, ma'am."

Mrs Morcom stepped back and sat heavily on her stool. "It was a snake that killed him," she said in a small, calm voice.

9

A VISIT TO
MISS LILLINGSWORTH

"I haven't thought about Charles's death for a long time," she said.

"I'm so sorry…" I faltered.

"No, no," she said. "You have nothing to apologize for."

"Should I – do you want – shall I ring for tea?"

"Do *you* want tea? After all, you're the one who saw…"

I shook my head.

"I would like to tell you about it, Verity. Can you bear it?"

"If you can, ma'am, I can."

"Charles and I had only been married six months, and we were on our first overseas trip. A sort of honeymoon, if a forty-year-old spinster can be allowed such romantic notions. We were staying with friends on Mount Macedon. That's in Victoria, my dear, in Australia." She paused, gathering her thoughts, and I thought her face seemed very old all of a sudden. "I had gone out sketching, and Charles was with me. I painted that bottlebrush – *Callistemon citrinus* is its botanical name – and then ... then we started walking back to the house. Charles stumbled over a stick. Or I thought it was a stick. When it went darting away, I realized it was a snake. It had bitten him on the leg and on the hand. He lost consciousness soon after, and died later that evening." She sat staring at me for a while, and then asked, "What exactly did you see, Verity?"

"I saw brightness. I heard a noise too – a kind of shrill piping."

"Cicadas," she said. "They are insects." She hesitated and then asked, almost shyly, "Did you see him? Did you see Charles?"

"No. Just the snake." I didn't tell her about the blackness and the misery.

She sat without speaking for a while, and then said, "My brother told me that you were a very special child. He was right. I am afraid for you, my dear." Mrs Morcom took my hand in hers. "Don't tell my brother, Verity. He will want to investigate and ... I believe some things are meant to stay hidden." She held my hand for a few seconds and then let it go.

"I'm very tired. I need to rest now."

"Yes, ma'am. Do you want me to help you up to your room?"

"No, dear. I'll lie down on the sofa."

When I looked back, she was sitting on her stool, very still, looking straight ahead at her painting. Antony and Cleopatra, in their case beside her, had rat-sized lumps halfway down.

At the side of the house there was a courtyard with an ivy-covered wall, a fish pond and a stone seat, where no one ever seemed to go. After leaving Mrs Morcom, that's where I headed. I needed to be on my own and think.

It was a fine day, but even sitting in the sunshine on the sun-warmed bench I felt cold. To tell the truth, I was scared. Nothing like that had ever happened to me before, and I didn't want it to happen again. If only I could go back to being an ordinary milliner's apprentice. But I knew I couldn't. During these last months at Mulberry Hill, what with the lessons, the experiments and the Confidential Inquiries, I knew that my life had changed for ever.

Mrs Morcom had said I was a very special child. Well, I had a special gift; there was no getting away from it. But surely finding lost things was special enough. It made me feel cheerful and useful and good about myself. This was awful. I'd seen something from another time, another place, a place half a world away. But what worried me most was that I'd seen it through someone else's eyes. Dead eyes. What if ... what if it happened all the time? Stands to reason half the things you touch or handle every day have been in a dead person's hands. I suddenly felt weak and wobbly.

"Verity! Verity, are you unwell?" I opened my eyes to find SP right in front of me. "What's wrong? You look as if you've seen a ghost."

"I think I have," I said.

He sat beside me on the bench. "What do you mean?"

"I was looking at one of Mrs Morcom's pictures, and it came to me – in my mind's eye – the snake and her husband..."

"Oh, no," he said. "Playing with cards and tokens was fine. Finding things – it's harmless, like a game. But this! Verity, please don't tell Father—"

"Don't tell Father what?" This quiet little spot where no one ever came had turned out as busy as Piccadilly Circus. Now the Professor was there, on the other side of the wall, peering at us through the ivy. He walked through the gate and into the courtyard. "What is it, Verity, that you're not to tell me?"

SP gave a big sigh. "Go on, Verity," he said. So I did.

"Ah, poor Charles." The Professor sighed very deeply. "Poor, poor Charles."

"Father," said SP, coming to stand behind the Professor and putting his hand on his shoulder.

"It's all right, my boy. The way forward is to observe," he said, almost as if speaking to himself. "To study and observe, to formulate our hypotheses, to test them against our observations, and then to devise carefully considered experiments."

Experiments? That was why Mrs Morcom didn't want him to know. Like SP said, cards and lost toasting forks were all very well, but this was playing with things that oughtn't to be played with.

"No experiments, Father," said SP, giving me a reassuring glance. "Verity was frightened."

"Frightened? Yes, I suppose she would be," he said absent-mindedly. Then he brightened up. "Verity, what you have just experienced is called Psychometry. From the Greek *psyche* – spirit or soul – and *metron*, measure. The term was coined by Joseph Buchanan about thirty years ago. He believed that all objects give off vibrations, and the psychic individual acts as a kind of mental sponge."

"Father, please stop. Verity doesn't want to be a sponge. Can't you see that she is distressed?"

113

The Professor looked at me properly. "I'm so sorry, Verity." He thought for a few seconds, and then his face brightened again. "Maria!" he cried. "I shall take you to see Maria Lillingsworth."

"Mr and Mrs Rhodes, Father," SP reminded him. "We are calling there to discuss their case at four."

"They're on the way, aren't they? Why, that's splendid. We can see Maria afterwards. I'll send her a note straightaway." He rubbed his hands together, beaming and nodding like his old self. "What d'you think, SP?"

"If you say so, Father," he said, but I could tell that he wasn't happy about it. He wasn't happy at all.

I dozed a little in the carriage on the way to Carisbrook Grove, and then when the Professor and SP went in to the house (I wasn't to come in, they said, for the Rhodes were a very old-fashioned couple, and might take exception to a female taking part in the investigation), I dozed a little more. It was a warm afternoon, and it was nice to lie against the padded leather seat. Before I knew it, I wasn't just dozing, I was asleep.

I was asleep, and watching my mother. She was stitching something. In my dream, I moved closer, and saw that it was white and soft. White velvet. Swags and folds of white velvet lay on her lap like

114

snow. There was a tangle of white fur trimming on the table beside her, and a fur hat too. Madame didn't make that sort (it was a furrier's job) but they were all the mode last winter. *À la Russe*, they were called. Russian hats. Ma's fingers were moving like lightning, and she was frowning with concentration, just the way I remembered. Suddenly, she looked up from her sewing and smiled.

"Verity?"

Ma vanished, and I was back in the carriage outside Mr and Mrs Rhodes's house. I sat up straight and tried to tidy myself up. I must have pulled at my clothes in my sleep, for my top button was undone and the lucky piece was hanging out.

"I'm sorry to wake you, my dear. We have finished with the Rhodes."

"I wish we never started," muttered SP.

"Quite so, my boy. And now it's time to go and see Maria."

Miss Lillingsworth's house was less than ten minutes away, but as I knew from my days delivering hats, streets can be close together and yet far apart in London. Carisbrook Grove was toffee-nosed and genteel, whereas Canning Street was a little bit shabby, and Miss Lillingsworth's house was the smallest and shabbiest in the row. She opened the door herself, wearing a big white apron.

"Saddy!" she said, holding out her hand to the Professor. It was bright purple, and I wondered if she was another artist. She looked down at it, then up at us, and explained, "I am helping Millie with the plums today."

"*Miss Maria*," a cross voice panted from behind her in the narrow passageway.

"Yes, Millie?"

"I'll answer the door, Miss Maria." Millie was large and red-faced and it was clear she bossed her mistress round like nobody's business. "Take your apron off now, and I'll bring your tea." She bobbed a curtsey to SP and the Professor, but she gave me the once-over as I walked in, and I knew by her stare that I didn't measure up. "If you'll be so good as to step in 'ere, sirs," she said, all but shoving them into the front parlour. "Miss," she added as an afterthought.

"You'll have to forgive Millie," said Miss Lillingsworth. "She's terribly embarrassed for me because I've been caught helping in the kitchen."

"We are early, and I'm sorry to have interrupted the plums. We spent much less time with our clients than I'd anticipated. Are *you* embarrassed, Maria?" asked the Professor.

"Of course not, Saddy. It's lovely to see you. And you must be Verity." She turned to me with a smile.

Miss Lillingsworth was a tall, thin, middle-aged lady with a lot of nose, not much chin, and such big teeth she could have eaten an apple through a picket fence. She was badly dressed, and very, very plain – but when she smiled, you forgot what she looked like. And her eyes were lovely.

"Saddy wrote me a brief note this morning, my dear, telling me you'd had an experience that worried and frightened you. Would you care to talk to me about it?"

I glanced at the Professor, and he nodded encouragingly.

"Yes, ma'am."

She waited for a few seconds, and then she nodded encouragingly too. But I didn't know what to say.

"You had an experience," she prompted.

I was embarrassed to find myself trembling and near to tears. The Professor spoke for me.

"It seems that Almeria was showing Verity some of her flower pictures. Verity had this particular one in her hands, and..." He turned and gestured for me to go on.

"It was horrible, ma'am," I whispered. "I felt like I was drowning under a black wave."

"You were in the water?"

It was so hard to explain. "It was a wave of feelings, ma'am. Hopeless and miserable and sad."

"And did you see anything?"

"Just bright light and a black thing sort of darting."

"The snake," said the Professor. "You remember poor Charles, don't you? Almeria had just sketched that very picture when it happened."

"I see." Miss Lillingsworth looked at me kindly. "Nothing like this has happened before?"

"No," I whispered.

The Professor couldn't keep quiet any longer.

"May I suggest an experiment, Maria?" He explained that he had with him a client's letter, and he proposed that Miss Lillingsworth and I both attempt a reading from it. His eyes sparkled with excitement. "The thing is, some subtle influence from Almeria may have affected Verity the other day. So this way we can compare——"

"Father," interrupted SP. "I think poor Verity is tired of experiments."

Miss Lillingsworth said nothing, but frowned to show she disapproved.

"What do you say, Verity?" the Professor asked. "It's entirely up to you."

The three of them stood, waiting for my answer.

118

I took a deep breath. "I'll do it," I said. With SP and Miss Lillingsworth on my side, I knew I didn't have to. But I didn't want to be scared of this new gift, and the way I saw it, the only way not to be scared was to find out more about it.

"You are a brave girl," said Miss Lillingsworth. She added, in a low voice, very gently, "There's no need to be frightened."

Frightened! My teeth were chattering. I only hoped I could go through with it.

Miss Lillingsworth got the Professor to draw the curtains and go and sit with SP on the window seat, and then we began.

"Place your right hand over the letter, shut your eyes, and just wait," she said. "Pictures or thoughts may float through your mind, or they may not. Don't force anything. Just wait."

I did as she told me. Nothing. My mind was a blank. I stopped feeling afraid. My stomach rumbled. A fly buzzed somewhere. And then – my fingers were tingling, and there was the sea and sand and children paddling and a donkey. Noises now too – laughter and the clip-clopping of horses' hooves, and a man's voice, just a murmur, and then a woman's replying, soft and low. "So 'appy," she said. "So 'appy."

10

THE SEVENTH STAR

I opened my eyes and looked up.

"Don't tell me," said Miss Lillingsworth. She shut her eyes and put her hand on the paper, and we waited. It was only about a minute before she opened her eyes again.

"That is that," she said. She shook her hands as if flicking off water, and then stretched them. "Now, Verity. Did you see anything?"

I breathed a sigh of relief. This was nothing like the last time. Nothing scary or horrible. In fact, it was a day at the beach.

"The sea," I said. "It was like that postcard Cook's cousin sent from Margate. And I heard voices. They were sweethearts."

"Why do you say that?"

"Well, he was talking sweet and low to her, but I couldn't make out the words, and she was saying she was happy." I thought some more. "They was in a carriage."

"Well," Miss Lillingsworth stood up, went over to the window and opened the curtains. "Well, well!"

"Well, well, what?" asked the Professor. "Did you get a reading, Maria?"

"I did. It was substantially the same as Verity's." Miss Lillingsworth stretched her hands again, cracking the joints. "I would say that the subject is alive and well and very happy indeed. I also think he has just married."

SP and the Professor looked at each other. "Good lord," said the Professor. "What does your conscience tell you to do, SP?"

"Return their fee and tell the Rhodes we cannot help them," said SP, promptly.

"I agree, my boy." The Professor explained briefly that he had been engaged by Mr and Mrs Rhodes to find their missing son and return him to them. They knew he was alive, for he'd sent them one brief letter, assuring them that all was well, and then they'd heard nothing more. The governess, coincidentally, had left their employment at around the same time.

"It's not her," I piped up.

"How do you know, Verity?" asked the Professor.

"She said 'so 'appy'. She drops her aitches, like

I did before Miss Judith taught me not to. No governess would speak like that. So at least you can tell his ma and pa it's not her."

"I don't want to tell them anything. Poor lad, he deserves his happiness. We'll let him escape, eh?"

"But what will they live on?" I asked. All three stared at me. "They can't be happy if they've got no money," I said. "He's a gentleman and all."

"Oh, Verity," sighed the Professor. "Now you have presented me with a moral dilemma."

"Beg pardon?"

Miss Lillingsworth put her hand over mine. "That is for you and SP to work out, Saddy. I want to talk to Verity." She stood up briskly and rang the bell. "Alone."

"But Maria, I wanted to ask Verity..." The Professor already had his notebook and pencil out, but Miss Lillingsworth shooed him and SP towards the doorway.

"Shall we come back in, say, ten minutes?" the Professor asked.

"I will call for you when I want you, Saddy."

The Professor patted my shoulder, and SP gave my hand a little squeeze. Then we were alone.

"Please make yourself comfortable," said Miss Lillingsworth. Which was hard to do on her horsehair sofa that was about as comfy as a rock. She sat on a straight-backed chair opposite me, and put her hands in her lap. "I shouldn't say it, my dear, but we shall do much better without Saddy. You know what I mean." If I didn't know she was such a lady, I'd swear she'd winked at me. "He always likes to jump in and be doing something when sometimes what you have to do is simply wait. You say you have never had a reading from an object or token before?"

"No, ma'am."

"But you have the ability to find lost things, I believe. How long have you had that?"

I thought carefully. "Always, I think, ma'am. I used to find Ma's bits and pieces when I was little, and then at Madame's, it was the same. I never thought about it much. She was very forgetful, was Madame."

"Has your gift changed lately in any way?"

"My fingers start to itch." I thought hard. "I get a bit more of a picture in my mind's eye than I used to. This thing with the painting and the snake, though – that's new, that is."

"It frightened you, I can see. And it came out of the blue? Unexpectedly?"

I nodded.

"Then something has initiated a new phase of psychic perception. Those experiments are the

123

most likely cause. It seems they are developing your psychic skills, in rather the way that practice on an instrument improves one's musical skills." She gave a gentle horsey smile. "Let me tell you something about myself. When I was in my late twenties, after a severe illness, I gained the ability to 'read' objects. The impressions would come at any time, in any place and, like you, I found them frightening and sometimes overwhelming. To tell you the truth, at first I thought I was going mad and didn't tell anyone. I prayed a great deal." She paused. "And then gradually I became aware that just as I had the power to receive these impressions, so did I have the power to block them out."

"How did you do it, ma'am?"

"I trained my mind. I would picture myself pulling down a window blind, so that the impression was hidden from view."

A blind. Would that do the trick for me? Perhaps I had better think of myself shutting the lid of a hatbox, or snipping off a length of ribbon.

She must have seen how I was frowning, for she said quickly, "You will find your own method, my dear. For some people, it is deep breathing. Just remember that you are not at the mercy of your talent. It is a gift, and you may be able to help people, to set their minds at rest." She made a floaty sort of gesture with her hands. "I use my gift as a service to mankind, and I never, never charge."

Charge? Whatever was she on about?

"Now, may I try to gain some impressions of my own?"

I said I didn't mind, and so Miss Lillingsworth held her hands about an inch away from my body, and ran them, without touching, all over my head, neck and chest.

"Ah!" she said. At the same moment that I felt a sharp tingle on my collarbone. She pointed to the spot. "What have you there? Is it a locket?"

"It's just a lucky piece," I said. "On a cord. Ma gave it to me."

"May I see it, please?"

I slipped it over my head and handed it to her. She held it on the flat of her palm and looked at it with a puzzled expression for a few seconds. Then she shut her eyes.

At first I watched her but that seemed rude, so I studied the clock on the mantelpiece instead. The clock ticked away and Miss Lillingsworth still had her eyes shut, so then I inspected her ornaments. She had a china cat and a bouquet made of shells and a very ugly pair of vases with peacock feathers in them.

I looked at her again. Her mouth was twitching slightly, but her breathing was now so slow and steady that I thought she'd fallen asleep.

"How many sisters do you have?" she asked abruptly, blinking her eyes open.

Before I could answer Millie poked her head in the door.

"Miss Maria, it's high time you had your tea," she said. "So I'm bringing it in now. Here come the gentlemen." And she waddled off towards the kitchen.

SP and the Professor came into the room, followed by Millie with the tea tray. When we were all settled with teacups, and bread and butter, the Professor couldn't hold back any longer.

"Anything to report, Maria?"

Miss Lillingsworth held out my lucky piece. The Professor briefly examined it, and then looked expectantly at Miss Lillingsworth.

"What do you know about the seventh son of a seventh son, Saddy?"

The Professor thought for a few seconds, and Miss Lillingsworth nibbled at a slice of buttered bread.

"A sort of mystical power has long been given to the number seven," he began, talking away as usual like he'd swallowed the dictionary. "The seven hills of Rome, Seven Ancient Wonders of the World, that sort of thing. The seventh son of a seventh son is supposed to be particularly lucky." He was warming up now, I could tell. "Indeed, he is supposed to inherit a miraculous power of—"

Miss Lillingsworth cut him off in full flood. "It isn't just the seventh son of a seventh son who has this reputation. It's less well known, but the seventh daughter of a seventh daughter is also believed to have special powers."

"Seventh daughter of a seventh daughter. How fascinating," said the Professor. He took out his little notebook and pencil and began to scribble, but Miss Lillingsworth put her hand on his arm and stopped him.

"Just listen, Saddy. Years ago I spent some time governessing in Orleans. That's in France," she said in an aside to me. "My employer, Madame de Puy, had five daughters and she was desperate for a son. She went to consult an old lady, Mère Lauriel, who was famous in the district. They called her a *septième étoile*."

"*Septième étoile?* A seventh star?" said the Professor. "What – or who – is that?"

"It is the seventh daughter of a seventh daughter," said Miss Lillingsworth patiently. I could see that she'd have been a good teacher.

"Please go on, Maria," said SP.

"A *septième étoile* may have a number of gifts. Mère Lauriel could see the future. But she told me that others can look back into the past. And some of them..." Here she turned to me. "Some of them, Verity, can find that which is lost."

"Ah," breathed the Professor. "I see."

"What happened?" I asked, still caught up in the story. "Did your employer have a son, after all?"

"She did. As a matter of fact, she had twins." Miss Lillingsworth held out my lucky piece again. "This is Verity's, Saddy. Her mother gave it to her. I recognized it as soon as I saw it. Mère Lauriel had a little medal just like this, engraved with the sign of the seventh—"

"The seven stars!" I burst out. So that was the point of Miss Lillingsworth's story. Could it be that my gifts – teleagtivism and psychometry, as the Professor would put it – were something handed down to me, mother to daughter, like family jewels? I thought of Ma, just after Pa died, feverish with typhoid. What did she know about the seven stars? My mind was whirling around so fast that it was hard to think or speak clearly. Or even speak at all. "Miss Lillingsworth, are you saying ... do you think ... am *I* a seventh star?"

128

She took my hand. "You have very special gifts. Now, tell me, how many sisters do you have?"

They were all watching me, kind and concerned, expecting an answer. And what could I tell them?

"I don't know."

"You don't know?" The Professor was taken aback. "What do you mean, you don't know?"

"I don't rightly know if I've got any sisters or not. You see, my uncle Bill told me something the day I left Madame Louisette's." I took a deep breath and got it over with. "He told me that I was a foundling left in a basket outside my father's shop. Ma and Pa adopted me for their own, and never told me nothing about it. They was –" I remembered Judith's grammar lessons at last, and I gulped back a sob as I corrected myself – "*were* the best, the kindest, the lovingest…"

A handkerchief was pressed into my hand. I blew into it, and straightened my shoulders.

"Verity, why didn't you tell me this?" asked the Professor.

"You never asked."

The Professor winced ever so slightly. But it was true. All he'd been interested in was his blessed experiments, not me.

"I'm sorry, Verity." He stared at his polished boots for a few seconds before he met my eye. "Harriet would be ashamed of me. She would have asked you about your family. She would have been kinder to you than I have been."

Harriet was the Professor's wife, who'd passed on three years ago. Judith had told me a bit about her. She sounded like she'd been very clever and very kind. The Professor blew his nose very loudly, and handed the lucky piece back to me.

"Did your mother tell you anything about this medallion, Verity?"

"No, she gave it me just before she died. I've kept it all this time." I held up the battered little piece. "I haven't got much to remember them by, you see."

"So," said Miss Lillingsworth. "Is it possible, Saddy, that you could find the identity of Verity's real mother?"

"Ma *was* my real mother," I said.

She gave me a sad smile. "Quite so, my dear."

"Why can't *you* help us to find Verity's birth mother, Maria?" the Professor burst in. "Surely the token would be enough to accomplish some kind of a reading?"

"I have held it already," she said. "I was receptive, and I received nothing clear. I sensed a long history, and many hands, and great sorrow. That is all."

"What about you, Verity? Have you tried?"

I put the lucky piece on my palm and closed my hand and shut my eyes and waited. Nothing. Nothing at all.

"It is clearly a case for the Confidential Agents," said Miss Lillingsworth. "Or for..." She turned to the Professor and whispered something in his ear. He turned to me with a serious expression on his face.

"That is for Verity to say," he said.

"But of course, Saddy."

"Verity, Maria would like you to go to a gathering with her."

"What sort of gathering, if you please, ma'am?"

"A seance."

Another word I didn't know. I looked from her to the Professor.

"A seance is a meeting of people who are seeking to communicate with the departed," he said. "Spiritualists believe that—"

SP broke in. "Please, Father. You promised."

I looked from one to the other. What were they talking about?

SP turned to me. "A seance is a meeting with the dead."

11

POISON PENS

I said yes. But that night when I was lying sleepless in my bed I began to wish I hadn't. This was getting in too deep. How many times had I longed for a word, just one loving word, from Ma since she'd passed? But when it came down to it, did I really want to speak to her? As far as I understood it, when you died you went up to heaven. And stayed there, "peacefully resting", as it said on Ma's gravestone. But Miss Lillingsworth seemed to think that dead people were all around us in some kind of spirit world. Just floating around. It didn't seem right nor natural.

The seance was in a week's time. I would have moped and fretted until then, and worn out the lucky piece with putting it on and off and staring at it as if it could talk. But that morning, the letters began.

The first one came from "a friend".

Verity Sparks,
Who do you think you are? Get back to the
gutter where you belong or something bad will
happen. That's a promise.
A friend

No address. It hadn't been posted, either — no stamp — so someone must have come up to the house and put it in the letterbox. But who? Miss Charlotte came to mind. She was the only person I could think of who'd bear me a grudge, and since I didn't care two hoots about her, I just screwed it up and put it in the rubbish where it belonged.

The next one came not to the Plush household, but to the Professor's cousin, Mrs Honoria Dalrymple. We only knew what was in it because that afternoon at teatime there was the sound of a carriage coming down the drive.

"Who could that be?" asked the Professor, looking up from the anchovy toast. "Have you invited anyone to tea, my dears?"

Before any of us could answer there was a tremendous banging at the door, and instead of waiting to be let in, a tall red-haired woman rushed into the room, huffing and puffing like an engine.

"Sit down, dear Honoria," said the Professor, pulling

up a chair for her. "You look close to an apoplexy."

"Explain this!" she cried, thrusting a letter at him. "It was hand-delivered this very morning, and I came as soon as I could." She turned and stared at me with a most unfriendly expression on her face. "And this, I suppose, is the young person, Verity Sparks?" She said my name like a horse had done its business right under her nose. All I could do was stand and curtsey, while she stood there breathing heavily, one hand clutched to her huge bosom. "Read it, Saddington."

Shaking his head, he began.

"*Dear Mrs Dalrymple, I am writing to you as one who holds family honour dear, and does not like to see RESPECTABLE people imposed upon by GUTTERSNIPES who are only out to feather their own nests and ensnare innocent and well-meaning people into entanglements which may prove DETRIMENTAL to their reputations.*

"*Did you know that your cousin's daughter, Miss Judith Plush, has as a constant companion, AND LIVING IN THE SAME HOUSE, a common young person, Verity Sparks, who was until a very short while ago a COMMON MILLINER'S APPRENTICE? She has WORMED her way into the Plush household. Your own reputation may even suffer from this UNFORTUNATE connection, and I cannot urge you too strongly, Mrs Dalrymple, to ACT!*

Yours, a well-wisher.

"Good lord, Honoria," said the Professor. "Is this a joke?"

"A joke! I think not."

"If not, it's a lot of nonsense." He screwed up the letter and threw it across the room into the fire. "Now that's out of the way," he said, "sit down and have some tea. Anchovy toast?"

Mrs Dalrymple glared at him, and then glared even harder at me. "Don't say I didn't warn you, Saddington. When you wake up murdered in your beds, don't come crying to me."

I could hardly believe my ears. Me, a murderer? Mrs Dalrymple may have been a relative, but she'd gone a step too far. I opened my mouth to say something, but the Professor put his hand over mine and squeezed it gently, shaking his head.

"It's not worth it," he whispered.

Mrs Dalrymple was only just hitting her stride. "It is dangerous to reverse the natural order by elevating inferior persons. It is irreligious as well. But what can I expect from a godless *scientist*?" More manure under her nose. "At least I know I have done my duty."

"What duty is that?" It was Mrs Morcom, coming

in late for tea as usual. She looked coolly at Mrs Dalrymple and held out a red and orange hand. "How are you, Honoria?" she said. "How's that girl of yours? Have the pimples cleared up yet?"

Mrs Dalrymple ignored her. "Be it on your own heads," were her parting words, and she turned on her heel and stalked out.

Mrs Morcom didn't seem to care a fig about Mrs Dalrymple or her letter, but when the Professor told her about the proposed seance she got very angry. She said they should not interfere with me, and that all of this spiritualist stuff was rubbish and wrong. They had a big argument, and the next day she packed her bags and went off on a sketching trip to Cornwall.

"That woman is impossible," spluttered the Professor after she marched out to the carriage, nose in the air, without so much as a wave goodbye. "If she thinks anyone will miss her, she's mistaken."

"I will," said Judith.

"And so will Amy," I said. I felt sorry for Mrs Morcom's dog, looking at me all lost and lonely with her big brown eyes, and so I began to take the poor thing for afternoon walks.

The Plushes' house, Mulberry Hill, is what they call a villa. The back of the property runs down to a little stream. There's a bridge that crosses over it, and from there you can walk along a lane that leads past the back gardens of the other villas. It was a pretty walk, and it got me out of the house, and so I got into the habit of taking Amy out most afternoons.

I was standing on the bridge, daydreaming a bit while Amy snuffled in the leaf litter, when I heard a voice call out my name.

"Miss Sparks!" It was Ben O'Brien, the gardener's boy, the one who bred the rats. He came panting up to me. "This come for you, miss," he said, holding out an envelope.

"Who gave it to you?"

"An ole woman."

"Did she say who she was?" Ben shook his head. "What did she look like?"

Ben shrugged. "Skinny. She had a shawl on."

A skinny old woman in a shawl. Ben would never make a confidential inquiry agent. I thanked him and he ran off. "Verity" was written on the front in big round letters. I opened it.

Dear Verity,

I am in truble. I need to see you. Dont com to me at madams, and dont tell anyone. I will

mete you on the canal walk near St Johns
church at five oclock on Wensday. Dont let me
down.

your,
Beth

Guiltily, I realized that I'd scarcely given Beth a thought lately. I'd been at Mulberry Hill over two months now, and though at first I'd missed her and Cook and Madame and the other girls something fierce, gradually I'd got so used to my new life that I'd almost forgotten about the old. What with the kindness of the Plush family and my book-learning and of course my job helping with confidential inquiries, my days were full and – I thought I'd never say it – happy. Poor Beth. What could be the matter? She wanted me to meet her tomorrow, and I wasn't going to let her down.

I called Amy. Even on this sunny afternoon, with the red and gold leaves fluttering from the trees and birds singing, I didn't feel like walking any more. I tucked the letter in my pocket and went back to the house.

Wednesday was another warm day, but by half-past

four, when I set out to the canal walk, the air was cooling and I was glad of my shawl. With Amy lolloping along beside me, it should have been another lovely walk through the leafy streets and lanes of St John's Wood. But I was worried. What was the matter with Beth? More importantly, how could I help her? If she needed money, I could give her three pounds. It was a lot of money, but would it be enough?

I knew I was right on time, for I heard the bells as I crossed the road at the church corner. Amy and I walked through a shrubby kind of lane to the canal. A couple of elderly ladies with small dogs passed by, then a clergyman with a worried look. Then no one for quite a few minutes, until a couple of boys flashed past, running and shouting, and a couple more dog walkers. Then it was quiet again. Minutes passed, and I waited. Then a quarter of an hour. Still I waited. No Beth. Had I got the time wrong? Or the day or the place? I took the letter out of my pocket and re-read it. I had come at five o'clock. This was the canal walk, right near the church. Where was she?

"Amy!" Her bark was so sudden and so loud that I dropped the letter.

"You silly dog, barking at nothing," I told her sternly. "Sit." She sat down, trembling and whining, and then the hair stood up on the back of my neck.

Someone was watching me. I knew it. I could *feel* it, and so could Amy. She strained at her leash. The lane behind me was dark and shadowy now, and the canal walk was deserted. There was a rustling noise in the bushes, and Amy barked again.

"Who's there?" I called.

Nothing.

"WHO'S THERE?" I was gooseflesh all over, but I wasn't going to show I was frightened. How dare someone lurk there trying to scare me? "This dog bites," I called. "So you'd better come out and state your business or push off!"

Nothing. Just that feeling of eyes on me. I was close to bolting when I heard someone coming along the canal walk, whistling. From inside the thicket of shrubs and small trees, I heard the crunch of footsteps on twigs and the rustling of leaves. Amy strained forward, barking like mad, and then a voice called from behind me.

"Miss Sparks. Good evening. Fancy meeting you here."

"Mr Opie!"

Silly Amy instantly lost interest in the watcher in the bushes. She bounced up to Mr Opie and licked his hands.

"Miss Sparks, are you quite well? You look—"

"I am perfectly well, Mr Opie. It's just … I got a letter from a friend asking me to meet her here, and she didn't turn up, and then I was sure I was being watched, and…" I knew I was babbling, but now that I was safe, I couldn't help it. "I'm so glad it's you."

"Here," said Mr Opie, taking me by the arm. "I think I'd better escort you home."

The family was in the drawing room.

"Opie, my dear chap," boomed the Professor. "Haven't seen you for ages. I missed you when you called last week. Come in. Come in." In the fuss and bother of offering a sherry, and Judith dropping the tray, and Amy jumping up and knocking over a pot of aspidistras, it was a little while before Mr Opie was able to come out with the real reason for his call.

"Someone was watching you?" asked the Professor. "Did you see who it was?"

"No, but someone was there. I could feel it."

"Have you still got Beth's letter?"

"No, I dropped it," I said. Then suddenly I remembered something. Beth was the youngest of thirteen children from Spitalfields. She was clever with her hands, but she'd never been to school. "Beth can't read or write. She didn't write that letter."

141

"She may have got someone else to write it for her," said SP.

Of course.

"Hmm," said the Professor. "Another letter. And hand-delivered, like the last."

"What other letter?" asked Judith.

"That most peculiar letter that Honoria brought us. It's been bothering me, you see. How I wish I hadn't burned it."

"I got another one as well," I confessed, and told them about it. "I thought it was probably from Miss Charlotte."

"Two poison-pen letters, and then this," mused the Professor. "We must ask ourselves, are all three connected?"

"Of course they are," said SP. "And we call ourselves inquiry agents! We need to investigate this without delay. Opie, will you come with me to the canal walk, to see if we can find the letter?"

"Of course."

"Don't worry, Verity," said the Professor. "Would you like it if tomorrow you were to visit Madame Louisette's? You could reassure yourself that your friend is not in trouble."

I smiled at him gratefully. If I could just see Beth, my mind would be at ease.

◆ ◆ ◆

The next day, Judith and SP took me into town and dropped me off at Madame's. They had business, they said, and would pick me up in an hour's time.

It was awkward. I could see Beth and Emily and Maria staring at my new clothes and boots with envy. We were different now, and there wasn't much to say.

When I asked Beth if she'd written me a letter, she gave me a funny look.

"What for?" she asked.

She was quite well, she said. Quite happy too, and she seemed fond of the new girl, Sallie, who was sharing her room. Madame was pleased to see me, but just as pleased to see me go. Cook was the only one who gave me a smile and a hug and a bit of a welcome. I left the workshop feeling sad and a bit lonely, like a stranger in my own life.

12

THE PEOPLE NEXT DOOR

Three letters. One to scare me, one to make the Plushes turn me out of the house and one to lure me out to the canal walk.

We had a bit of a conference about them the morning after I went to Madame's.

"We have no evidence," said the Professor. "We can't compare them, or inspect the paper, the ink or the penmanship. Bother! It was so careless of me to throw it into the fire. If only you'd kept the first one, Verity."

"If only we'd found the last one, down by the canal," said SP.

"Do you think they are all from the same person?" I asked. "From Miss Charlotte maybe?"

The Professor and SP shared a look, and I could see that we'd all been thinking the same thing.

SP said, "Miss Charlotte is a strong possibility. Opie and I are investigating."

"I do not think you are in any danger, Verity," added the Professor. "But don't go wandering off by yourself until we get to the bottom of this."

"I won't."

Silly of me, but I felt the pricking of tears in my eyes. I'd looked after myself for so long that it gave me a funny sort of feeling to see those two so careful and concerned. I could fight my own battles if I had to, but it was good to have help.

That afternoon, when Judith went next door to visit her friend, I went too.

"Mr Tissot is an artist," Judith told me. "He's French. He's quite famous, and very amusing."

"And Mrs Tissot?"

"Kathleen's a dear," she said warmly.

We found them out in the garden. He had his easel set up under some trees next to an ornamental pond, and was painting a portrait. The model was right in front of him. It was Mr Opie.

"Oh," said Judith. "You!"

Mr Opie went white, Judith went red, and I felt embarrassed for the pair of them. Mr Tissot didn't seem to notice a thing.

"Judith, you're just in time. I need you to read to Daniel, or talk to him, or sing to him – anything, mademoiselle, to keep him from fidgeting. No, you can't refuse – it will be just for ten minutes – I need the angle of his wrist to be just so." Mr Tissot was a small dark gentleman, about forty, with a strong accent. "Kathleen, *chérie*, give Judith your book." I turned, and saw a lady lying in a kind of long net strung between two trees. She had a book in her hand, but it was upside down.

"She's quite useless at entertaining him," said Mr Tissot in a teasing voice. "Reading puts her to sleep."

With a laugh, she threw the book at him, and then beckoned me over. "How rude they are." Her voice was husky and low, Irish-sounding, and now that I was up close I could see that she was very pretty, with dark brown curls and bright brown eyes and a lively heart-shaped face. Her hat, a tip-tilted straw trimmed with red silk poppies, was what Madame would call *très chic*. "But I suppose art comes before everything else, even manners," she said.

I didn't know how to answer that, so I curtseyed, and murmured, "How d'you do?" as Judith had taught me.

"You're not the one with bad manners. Perhaps I am, for teasing you so. I am Kathleen. And you are?"

"Verity Sparks, ma'am."

"Well, Verity Sparks, can you help me out of this

hammock?" She clasped my hand, and by swinging the net sideways I managed to tip her out onto her feet. She laughed again, but then she coughed and I saw how thin she was, and how the veins in her wrists and hands stood out as if they'd been drawn on with blue ink. She stood holding my hand for a few seconds, breathing heavily, and then said, "Judith told me you were visiting. You are a friend of the family?"

That's what the Plushes had been telling people. It was simpler than going into the experiments and the confidential inquiries. "Yes, ma'am," I said.

"No, no, don't call me ma'am; it makes me feel as old as the hills. You call our friend over there 'Judith'; call me 'Kathleen' and then I'll feel as young as she is." She looked across at Judith. "Dear Judith," she said, and her voice was very gentle. "She's a darlin' girl. But so unhappy. You know, Verity, there are many obstacles for the respectable. Almost as many as there are for the thoroughly bad. Shall we have some lemonade and cakes, just you and me?"

"Yes, please, ma'am," I said happily.

Kathleen Tissot was a little strange. With her playful ways, she was more like a girl my age than a grown-up lady, but I liked her at once.

"Oh," she said, glancing over my shoulder. "Here is another visitor."

Who should it be but Mr Savinov, wearing a pale linen suit and a shady hat, with a bunch of yellow chrysanthemums in his hand? I smiled and waved to him.

"It's darling Pierre. Shall we invite him to join our picnic?"

"Oh, yes." I liked his noble lion's head and kindly manners. It was a treat to see him again.

"We meet again, Miss Sparks." He bowed over my hand, and kissed Kathleen's. "How are you, Kathleen? What a ravishing hat."

"You're a flatterer, old friend. Have you come to see how the portrait's getting on?"

"I've come to see you, of course. But I may as well take a look." He turned to me. "It is a likeness of my son, you see."

"Mr Opie's your son?" I was astonished.

"No, no," said Kathleen. "Daniel is merely providing the body. Alexander is Pierre's son. He posed for the head months ago, but we were never able to get him to sit still after that."

"It's true," said Mr Savinov. "Alexander must be always in motion." He smiled as he walked with us to the terrace where chairs and a table and tea things were

148

set out. Kathleen went in search of cakes, and he leaned closer to me and said in a low voice, "I hope the meeting the other night did not tire you or distress you?"

I shook my head.

"You have remarkable abilities, Miss Sparks. Finding lost things – this is a truly useful gift." He sounded sad. "But things are not so important, I find. It is people who are. Can you find lost people, Miss Sparks?" He didn't wait for me to answer, but continued in a chatty tone. "And how are all at Mulberry Hill today?"

"We're very well, thank you," I said. "Even the snakes."

"Ah," he said. "Antony and Cleopatra, the fatal lovers of the Nile!"

Lovers of the Nile. I didn't understand what he meant but I did know that pythons weren't fatal unless they squeezed you to death. I was starting to explain this to Mr Savinov when Kathleen came back followed by a maid with a plate of little iced cakes.

"What are you two talking about so seriously with your heads together like that?" she asked.

"Snakes, my dear Kathleen," replied Mr Savinov. "We were talking about snakes."

"There are no snakes in Ireland, you know. Our darlin' St Patrick shooed them all out."

"Then they all went to Canada," he said. "One day, many years ago in Manitoba, Alexander somehow stumbled into a den of garter snakes – they sleep all winter, you see, in holes in the ground – and he fell in among thousands and thousands of little snakes all tangled up together waiting for the spring. He screamed like a ... like a..."

"Like a banshee," suggested Kathleen.

"Did he get bitten?" I asked.

"No, no. They were too sleepy, and I am not sure that their bite is dangerous, anyway. But Alexander never forgot his adventure. He still jumps at a coil of rope, or a worm."

"It's amazin' what can scare a person," said Kathleen. "Imagination can be a mighty dangerous thing."

"Imagination." Mr Tissot, smelling of oil and turpentine, strolled over to join us. "Where would we be without it?"

"A lot better off," said Mr Savinov.

"You can't believe that," said Mr Tissot, but Mr Savinov shook his head very sadly, and Kathleen tactfully changed the subject.

"I suppose Canada was very wild, Pierre?" she said. "The people as well as the places?"

"Not all." He laughed. "Montreal, where I lived for

many years, is a very fine old city, very cultured, very French. And Toronto has many splendid buildings, and an opera house…" He stopped, as if in a dream, and then caught himself up again. "Canada, though young indeed compared to Mother Russia, is very like it in some ways. It is wild and uncivilised in places, and poor Alexander did not have the gentlest of upbringings. When we came to England, I was determined to make him into an English gentleman." He shrugged his shoulders. "Now, I wonder what for?"

"Alexander is restless," said Mr Tissot. "Have patience. He doesn't yet know who he is."

"You are kind, James," said Mr Savinov.

What with laughing and having lemonade and tea and cakes, we passed another half an hour, and then Judith kissed Kathleen and said we must go. We were back in the orchard when she turned to me.

"I've still got the book."

"We can go back," I said. "It will only take a few minutes."

"Oh, will you take it back for me?" she said. "I don't want anyone to think … to think that…"

To think that you can't stay away from Mr Opie? I didn't say that, of course.

"I'll run back," I offered, and held out my hand for the book.

They were all still sitting out by the pond, so I gave the book to Mr Tissot and quickly walked away. In the lane I slowed down again. Little birds were hopping and calling and eating the last of the berries in the hedges. The autumn sun was still warm, the sky was blue, and it felt as if the whole world was a sunlit, peaceful place. Being city-bred, I'd never known much peace and quiet. I stood daydreaming for a moment, and then, out of the blue, there was that feeling again. It was the same as when I'd been waiting for Beth on the canal walk. I was being watched.

I spun around. There were trees on either side of the lane, and I could see their leaves trembling. Imagination, I told myself sternly. Like Kathleen said, it can be a dangerous thing. Why, a person could scare herself half to death when it's just little birds. Then I heard another sound. It sounded like a cough. Birds don't cough.

"Judith?" I whispered.

With a whirring of tiny wings, a flock of birds shot out from the bushes, chirping and chirruping. What had disturbed them? Was it a cat? And what was that? It sounded like someone's foot crunching on a twig.

Panicking now, I called, "Judith!"

"I'm just here, Verity." She moved into view, and I walked towards her. Another twig snapped somewhere behind me, and I broke into a trot.

"Oh, Judith!"

"There was no need to run," she said. "Was ... was Mr Opie still there?"

"Yes."

She gave a shy smile, followed quickly by a frown, and then walked ahead of me back to the house.

I followed slowly. Every now and then I glanced back. It *must* have been my imagination. I was just twitchy, I told myself, after that business with the letter. No one was there.

13

THE SEANCE

Perhaps it was the fog that put a dampener on things. After days of autumn sun the weather had changed, and when we left for the seance on Thursday night, a chill mist was settling. At first it was as wispy as the veiling on a lady's bonnet, but as we drove closer to the city it turned into fog. Like a blanket, I thought. Or a shroud.

It wasn't really like me to think about shrouds, but I'd been as jumpy as a cat all day and now I was feeling downright miserable. I wasn't the only one. Judith was moping about like a wet hen, the Professor had come down with a head cold that kept him tucked up with lemon drinks and hot water bottles, and even SP wasn't his usual self. But he tried to cheer me up. He told me all about Cleopatra's interesting condition – she had eggs, six of them – and how he'd seen the Prince of Wales in our street last week, and that there was a new case to work on. A problem with a will. I'm afraid I wasn't really listening, and we both fell silent. SP sighed. It was a long, heavy sigh.

"It's time I told you something, Verity." But he didn't.

"Have you found out who wrote those letters?" I asked him after a bit.

"No, no. Nothing like that. It's about us."

"Who?"

"Us. The Plush family," he said impatiently, as if I was being deliberately stupid. "Oh, I'm sorry, Verity. I just wish that we were not going to this seance tonight."

"Me too. Why don't we get John to turn back and have a quiet night at home?"

He smiled, and then shook his head. "We promised we'd call for Maria. And I told Father I'd take you, since he's laid low with this cold." Another great big sigh, and he began.

"Three years ago we were living in Cambridge. Cambridge is a town, but it's also the name of a university. Father had just been elected Professor of Astronomy there. I had nearly finished my law degree; Judith was just out of Miss Mitten's Academy for Young Ladies. And then this strange thing happened."

"What thing?"

"Early one morning, Father saw my mother walking by the river. She was dressed in one of her prettiest dresses, and she smiled and waved to him."

What was so strange about that? I wondered.

As if to answer my question, SP continued, "Father was running to fetch the doctor, Verity. For at that very moment, Mother was at home, in bed, dying."

A shiver ran right through me. Goose walking on your grave, Cook used to call it.

SP sighed. "Father believed that Mother, at the point of death, was thinking of him, and thus appeared by the river. After that, he became obsessed with the idea of life after death. He went to seances and readings; he consulted psychics and mystics and mediums. I believe some were genuine, but others were out-and-out frauds, only Father couldn't see it. He resigned from the university and devoted himself to the study of the supernatural. His university friends thought he'd gone off his head, and urged him to keep his project secret, but he wouldn't listen. It took its toll on his health, and finally ... finally Father was quite ill. We moved here and gradually he became more like himself again. He was able to recognize the frauds at least, and exposed several of them. Did you ever hear of the Frascati sisters? Or Ariel

Smoot? That's how the Confidential Inquiry Agency began. He has continued to conduct experiments in perception and intuition, and write scientific papers on them. But this new ability of yours, this psychometry ... we're back with the dead, and..."

I was glad that SP had told me about his father. Now I understood him a little better. And SP too. "And you're worried about him, aren't you?" I said.

"Not just him." SP sounded grave. "I am also worried about you."

We picked up Miss Lillingsworth and then drove to the house where the meeting was to be held. I don't know what I'd imagined – some shabby side street, perhaps – but it turned out that it was in Mayfair. Mayfair is a very posh address. I knew that 'cos some of Madame's best clients – big orders, late payments – lived there. We were being ushered in by a snooty manservant when I felt a tug at my elbow.

"Spare a penny, miss?"

It was a child. Too young to be out alone on a night like this, she was barefoot and dressed only in a light summer dress. Her arms were as thin as chicken bones and her eyes seemed huge in her little white face.

"Be off with you," said the footman, shooing her

157

like you'd try to scare off a pigeon, but the girl looked up at me with her big eyes.

"Please, miss." SP turned towards her and she flinched, as if expecting to be hit. "Please, sir, I only…"

"What's your name, dear?" asked Miss Lillingsworth.

"Polly."

"Here you are, Polly," said Miss Lillingsworth.

The little girl stared. Then she darted forwards, snatched the coin out of Miss Lillingsworth's hand, and ran.

"There's gratitude for you," muttered the footman. "Filthy little beggar."

"Through no fault of her own," snapped Miss Lillingsworth. I thought she was going to give him a lecture on charity, but she changed her mind. "Are we early?" she asked.

"No, ma'am," he said. "You are expected. Will you come this way?" He led us to the Red Drawing Room, and left us to wait for Lady Skewe and the medium.

The medium was called Mrs Miller, Miss Lillingsworth told us, and she was new to the Mayfair Spiritualist Circle.

"Mediums generally operate in a similar way,"

158

Miss Lillingsworth said. "Guests at the seance sit in a circle around a table and hold hands. The room will be darkened, and then it's simply a matter of waiting for the medium to go into a trance. The spirits of the departed—"

"Dead people," interrupted SP.

"That was in bad taste, SP," said Miss Lillingsworth, sounding every bit the governess. "As I was saying, they usually speak to the medium through a spirit guide or control. Madame Fustanella's was a druid called Orloc, but I believe Mrs Miller has a Scotchman." SP snorted, and she grinned. "Poor SP. Shall you sit out?"

"No, no. I might need to translate."

It was Miss Lillingsworth's turn to snort. "We will ignore him. Mrs Miller's spirit guide is called Doctor Proctor, and Lady Skewe tells me he *is* rather hard to understand sometimes, especially when he gets excited – he becomes quite vernacular."

I was still pondering the word "vernacular" when two ladies walked into the room. I picked Mrs Miller at once. She looked just like I expected – pale, with a widow's peak, trailing veils and shawls and ropes of jet beads.

"Lady Skewe, how kind of you to let us come," said Miss Lillingsworth, rising to greet her.

So I was wrong. I stared at the elegant young

woman who followed in Lady Skewe's wake. She was more like a fashion plate than my idea of a medium. She was wearing a ruffled peach-coloured dress with a little draped bustle, a tip-tilted evening hat that Madame would have been proud of, and neat boots with fancy buttons. She was holding the arm of a tall, whiskery man in smart evening clothes. He had the most magnificent moustache I'd ever seen, even bushier than SP's false one, and a funny round glass thing squinted into one eye.

"And this is Colonel Jebb, Mrs Miller's cousin," said Lady Skewe.

"Pleased to meet you," boomed the Colonel.

"Pleased to meet you," murmured Mrs Miller.

Though she was a real English rose, with blonde hair and a pink-and-white complexion, she didn't sound English at all. SP came forward and bowed over her hand.

"Do you mind me asking whereabouts in America you hail from, Mrs Miller?"

"From Baltimore, sir," Colonel Jebb answered for her, and she repeated it, very softly. She had a soft, flat, girlish sort of voice, and though she didn't seem shy, she clearly didn't have very much to say for herself. I hoped Doctor Proctor was a bit more talkative or the seance was going to be as flat as one of Cook's sponge cakes. I'd been a bit anxious before, but now … well, Mrs Miller was so ordinary that it seemed just a tiny bit silly.

We sat down in awkward silence, and then the manservant showed in two more guests. They were Mr Egg, a short tubby man who was trembling before we'd even started, and a French lady called Madame Dumas. She looked very stylish in a maroon silk evening gown that set off her dark hair and eyes. I noticed those eyes. They darted restlessly all over the room.

"Shall we begin?" said Lady Skewe brightly, for all the world as if we were going to play cards. The gas was turned down to a dim blue glow, and we sat, holding hands, waiting. All except Colonel Jebb – he was the recorder for the session.

It was quicker than I'd thought it'd be. Mrs Miller tilted her pretty face slightly upwards, closed her eyes and slumped forward. In a deep, growly voice she demanded, "Who's he?"

"Who is who, Doctor?" asked Lady Skewe.

"There's a one among ye who'd rather not be," said Mrs Miller. Or Doctor Proctor, I suppose I should say. "And to tell ye the truth, I'd rather he not be too. Tell him to sit by fire. Sit by the fire, and watch and listen. Then he can write it all up for his casebooks."

There was a cackle of not very nice laughter. "What volume are ye up to, laddie? Three? Four?"

SP changed places with Colonel Jebb, and I couldn't tell if he was disappointed or not. I clasped Madame Dumas's cold hand in mine. After a few seconds' silence, the doctor spoke again.

"Well, there are a few of ye here tonight, and there'll be taking turns or I'll have a word to say about it, indeed I will. Tubsy? Is Tubsy there?"

Mr Egg quivered. "Mother?"

"She wants to know why ye've not married. Tubsy, she says, there's Clara Claringbold very fond of ye and a most suitable wife in spite of the height difference. She wants to see grandchildren at Coddle Court. She wants lots of grandchildren."

"Yes, Mother." Poor Mr Egg was quivering like a jelly.

"She only wants ye to be happy, she says. She only wants what's best for ye. That other young person would never have been right for ye. It would have been a shameful connection."

At this point, Mr Egg began to cry.

"Chin up, Tubsy, she says. Be a man. And she says, look into Great Southern Consolidated. Buy shares now: by Thursday there'll be a run on them, and ye'll have missed out."

"Yes, Mother."

Mrs Miller sighed, and her head fell sideways. In the dim lamplight, she looked very pale.

"Palmyra? Palmyra!" Mrs Miller rapped the table, and Lady Skewe sat up to attention. Doctor Proctor was off again, talking quickly in that dry and scratchy voice and rolling his Rs. It seemed that Lady Skewe's mother was most concerned that her daughter's servants had let moths get into the linen cupboards. And silverfish in the library, and black beetles in the kitchen. Then suddenly, Doctor Proctor asked, "Does Verity remember the ragbag?"

The ragbag. It was just the tiniest wisp of a memory, but I seemed to be on the floor, with scraps of colour and softness scattered all around me. Velvet, I realized, and silk and satin. Just like the little quilt Ma had given me.

"Ma? Oh, Ma..." I could hardly speak from trembling. "Is it you, Ma?"

"Well, who do you think?" asked the doctor, crossly. "You were just a wee baby, she says, but how ye loved the ragbag. Ye used to take the pieces and stroke them and rub them to your bonny wee cheeks." The doctor's voice broke off, and Mrs Miller began to wheeze. The Colonel, who was sitting next to her, wiped her forehead with a handkerchief.

"She wants to know have ye got the lucky piece?" The doctor's voice was hoarse and urgent. "And have ye got the ring?"

"Yes, Ma. I have them now." I let go of the hands and undid my top button. I'd put the ring on the cord with the lucky piece, and worn them both round my neck especially, in case Mrs Miller was able to read tokens. "They're here. I have them here."

"It was for luck, she said when she gave them to you. She says she promised, she said she would never break a promise, and she loved ye as if you were her own. She loves ye still, and she watches over ye, and she is so proud."

"Ma," I was close to crying. "I miss you so much."

Then in a whisper, the doctor said, "*C'est pour toi, ma petite* ..."

"Oh," said Madame Dumas, and she gripped my hand hard. "A message for me."

"... *la Belle Sauvage*..."

Mrs Miller was struggling to breathe. She began to cough so hard that the Colonel put his arms around her and helped her to an armchair near the fire, where she lay back, panting.

"Richard," she said in her own flat, childish voice. "Won't you get me my drops? In my purse there..."

The Colonel did as she asked, saying, "It's the cold, and this infernal fog. What d'you Britishers call it? A pea souper. She gets bronchitis, you see."

Lady Skewe brought her a drink of water, and then turned to the rest of us at the table. "That must be enough for this evening." Looking really worried, she watched Mrs Miller for a few seconds, but as the lady was getting pinker, and breathing easier, Lady Skewe announced, "I will ring for tea."

Colonel Jebb took Mrs Miller away before the tea came. Being American, perhaps they didn't have the same need for it. Now the gas was turned up, and the rest of us stood around rather awkwardly. I could see tear streaks on Mr Egg's face, and I'm sure mine was the same. I realized that with all of SP's talk about frauds and charlatans, I hadn't quite expected Mrs Miller to be genuine. But the ragbag – it was something only Ma would know about. And what had the doctor said? "She loves ye still, and she watches over ye, and she is so proud." Perhaps tonight's messages would seem comforting in time, but for now, I was in a bit of a daze. I got a fright when Madame Dumas came right up to me.

"Dear child, you are blessed. Your mother talked to you tonight, eh? That is beautiful, so beautiful."

Her eyes glittered. She pointed to the cord round my neck and leaned forward. "Some special souvenirs, no? A ring – how rare, how lovely – and what is this?" She was so close now that she was touching me, and to my surprise she took the lucky piece between her finger and thumb and stared at it. Just as well the cord was long, or she'd have strangled me. I must have looked a bit surprised, for she backed off and said, "Wonderful, no? Your mother, she speaks to you, from beyond the gulf of death..." She waved her hands in a vague gesture, smiling, and didn't finish what she was saying to me. Instead, she turned to Lady Skewe.

"A thousand apologies, Lady Skewe," she cried. "Alas, I cannot stay for the tea. *Au revoir.*"

She practically bolted out of the room as a trio of maids, under the direction of the butler, came in with tea trays and we all sat down again.

"What a pity Madame Dumas could not stay." Lady Skewe shoved a dainty cake into her mouth. "I wonder what her message meant?"

"It's for you, little one," translated Miss Lillingsworth. "And then *la Belle Sauvage.*"

"The beautiful savage," murmured Lady Skewe.

"Or the savage beauty," said SP. "I wonder who she is."

"Perhaps no one," said Mr Egg. "*La Belle Sauvage* is the name of an old inn on Ludgate Hill. I believe it is in Seacoal Lane."

Then maybe the message was for me. That's where I used to live.

14

A VOICE IN THE DARK

I was very tired. Tea and cakes went on for ever, and so did Lady Skewe's loud voice pondering over moth and silverfish, and Mr Egg's endless teary stories about his mother. It was nearly an hour and a half later when we said our good-nights, and even then there was a last-minute delay while we waited for John.

"Where can he be?" SP was on the point of asking one of Lady Skewe's servants to go looking for him when the familiar carriage came around the corner and we got in.

I didn't feel like talking. None of us did. I was so caught up in thinking about Ma and Mr Egg and Seacoal Lane that I got a shock when I heard SP's voice, quite loud, calling to the coachman.

"John! I say, John." He rapped on the side of the carriage. "John." The carriage didn't stop, and he turned to Miss Lillingsworth and me. "We've been travelling for at least a quarter of an hour, haven't we? We should be near the bridge by now. What's got into the man? John!" The carriage stopped. "Perhaps he's taken a wrong turn in this fog. I'll get out and see what's the matter. Won't be a second." And with a reassuring nod, he jumped out.

"Where are we, I wonder?" asked Miss Lillingsworth. As far as I could see, with all the fog swirling around, we were in a narrow street between tall brick buildings. "We seem to be in some kind of business district. Are these warehouses, do you think?"

"Could be anywhere," I said. "Easy enough to get lost in this fog."

I could only make out bits and pieces of what SP said – "Why didn't you...? Who told you...?" – and John's low replies. Then there was a loud noise, as if something hit the side of the carriage.

Both of us froze, straining to hear. Miss Lillingsworth put her fingers to her lips and motioned for me to open the door. As quietly as we could, we slipped out of the carriage. There were no voices now. No sound at all. What had happened to SP? What had happened to John? Miss Lillingsworth clasped my hand, and the two of us moved forwards.

"Oh," Miss Lillingsworth gasped. My heart dropped like a stone. There was SP lying on the cobbles, with a caped figure bending over him. And it wasn't John. John is short and stout, and this man was tall and broad-shouldered. He looked up, and though I couldn't see properly, I knew he was staring straight at me. Miss Lillingsworth's calls of "Help! Help! Robbers!" seemed to disappear, muffled in the fog. I couldn't see his face, and that only made it worse when he spoke to me. His voice was deep, and smooth as black velvet – a gentleman's voice – but somehow not quite.

"Miss Sparks, I presume?" He held out his hand.

I panicked. Maybe I should have stayed with SP and Miss Lillingsworth, but I knew – I don't know how I knew, but I did – that this was no robbery. It was me he was after. I ran.

"Stop!"

Not bloody likely. I took off like a greyhound after the lure. Sure enough, footsteps followed, and that voice in the dark calling my name. I ran like the devil was after me along the deserted street, through an alley with a gas lamp at the far end, into a courtyard, and then down a lane into another court. The footsteps kept coming, and I ran all the faster. I turned a corner, and there was a light up ahead, shining red in the fog, and voices. It was a small fire, with ten or fifteen people around it.

"Help!" I called. "Help me." But almost at once I knew I'd picked the wrong mark. The faces that turned towards me were something out of a nightmare, all blooming with sores and bruises, teeth missing, eyes glittering. I could smell their stinking rags and the gin on their breath.

"Where are you going to, my pretty maid?" said one, and the whole company laughed.

Hands grabbed at me, clutching at my skirt and shawl. Fingers dug into my arms and poked my ribs. The nightmare faces leaned close to mine, but I pulled free and kept running.

I darted down another alley. There were more people here, and I hesitated in front of a group of women gathered around the entrance steps to one of the houses. A crew of small children was crawling and toddling around their skirts. Mothers with children, I thought. They'll help me.

"Excuse me..." I faltered.

"*Excuse me!* 'Ere's Lady Muck wants us to excuse 'er, girls," shrieked one.

"Excuse me. Excuse you," said another, and then the lot of them were screaming and cackling like witches, and the children were laughing too.

I kept running. More lanes, more alleys, more courts. Sometimes the fog was so thick I could hardly

171

see, and then it would lift and I'd realize how utterly lost I was. It was like a maze. Was I back where I'd started? I slipped and fell, and while I was lying winded I heard the voice, faint but following, still calling my name. "Verity Sparks, Verity Sparks!" I scrabbled myself up and kept going.

I had a stitch now, and I knew I couldn't go much further. I slipped again, this time landing on my back. I would have just lain there in the filth, except a hand grabbed me and pulled me sideways into the shadows. I struggled, but a dozen hands were on me. A voice said, "Shh. Yer safe," and when I looked, there was a mob of children leaning over me. Boys or girls, I couldn't tell; they were all pale as mushrooms, filthy, with matted hair. There were about ten of them, all huddled in the damp entrance to a cellar.

"Down there," ordered one of them, and half-pushed me down the steps. I crouched, he leaned on top of me, and the others crowded in front while the littlest one called, "Eh, mister. You after that girl?"

"Did you see her? Where did she go?" The velvet voice was hoarse and panting now.

"I seen 'er, sir. She went through the court and up the lane to the footbridge, sir. That way. Runnin' pretty fast."

"Good boy." I heard the jingle as a coin hit the

ground, and then the footsteps took off again, ringing on the cobbles, fainter and fainter, until they faded to nothing.

"Let 'er up." The crush of bodies moved off me and I poked my head up above the cellar. The court was quiet and empty.

"'E's gone." Now my eyes were used to the dark, I could see that the thin face was smiling. "Dirty ole man. We 'ates that, don' we? Dirty ole men, chasin' kids. They orter get the chop, we finks."

One of them made a cutting movement with his hands and the others nodded. I looked at them, all cuddled together like puppies. "Who are you?" I asked.

"I'm Dookie," said my rescuer. "An' this is Sam, Ella, Dobbin, Mike…" Each child bobbed its head. "An' this is Finn, and Eli, an' Gammy, an' Polly…"

"Polly." It was the little girl from outside Lady Skewe's.

"I tole you I seen 'er," she said to Dookie. "She was wiv the lady wot give me the deuce." She winked at me, and then asked in a hoarse voice, "You orright?"

"I am," I said. "Thanks to all of you. I think you've saved my life."

They giggled and squirmed a bit at that, and I glanced at the rotten steps and the splintered wooden door and the nest of old rags and newspapers. "Do you live here?"

Dookie nodded. "This is Flash Harry's place, where 'e takes 'is stuff. 'E lets us be 'ere 'cos we keep an eye. We see who comes an' goes and we lets 'im know. An' no one moves us on. You sure you're orright now, miss?"

"Yes."

"Well, you don' belong 'ere," said Dookie. He spoke kindly though. "You get you 'ome."

"Yes. I will. Thank you. Thank you all." Thank you seemed not quite enough. I didn't have any money on me. What else could I give them? "Could you use my shawl? It's muddy, but that will brush off. It's very warm." I held it out, and Dookie solemnly took it from me.

"We can use it. Where d'you want to go, miss? We can point you the way."

"I want to find a policeman." They laughed. Policemen were not their friends. "Or someone who can help me."

"That way. Through the alley and then keep goin' straight, and you'll hit the shops. There's lights an' there's cabs, an' this old preacher man on the corner sometimes. 'E might help. Bye, miss."

I ran at first, and then I walked. I felt almost safe,

174

for the lanes here were lit up and alive with people. They were loitering, or walking along like me, or just leaning in the shadows in doorways and porches, talking and drinking and smoking pipes. I thought that no one would be interested in a girl if she just walked along as if she knew where she was going, not showing that she was scared or lost. Well, I was almost right. I had my eyes fixed on the gas lamps up ahead, I suppose, for I walked right into a group of young men. One of them caught me by the sleeve, another grabbed my skirt, and they spun me round from one to the other, breathing beery fumes into my face.

"Let me go."

"Let me go," one of them said in a high squeaky voice, and they all laughed. "Who says?"

"Bill Bird," I said. I'll never know where that came from. It was probably the only time my uncle had ever helped me in his whole life.

"Bill Bird," one of them muttered doubtfully. "*The* Bill Bird?"

"Yes, *the* Bill Bird," I said firmly. "He's me uncle."

They drew back, and one of them said, "What you doin' 'ere then?"

"A spot o' business, and never you mind what it is, neither," I snapped, losing the genteel tone Miss

Judith had been working on. "Lemme go now, and I won't say nothin' about it to Uncle Bill. What's that street up ahead?"

They'd already scarpered, but the answer came floating back to me. "Haymarket."

Cook had always warned us about Haymarket, with its pubs and theatres and saloons that were open till all hours, full of shady characters just waiting to pounce on young girls. Was I out of the frying pan and into the fire? I turned the corner and looked around me. It was certainly crowded, busy and noisy. There were drunks of both sexes and painted ladies and beggars and jugglers and flower sellers and muffin men and an organ-grinder and even a few gentlemen too, in dark coats and stiff white collars and tall top hats. One of them laid his gloved hand on my arm, saying, "Hello, my dear. Going my way?" but I ducked away from him. I looked high and low for a member of the Metropolitan Police but I couldn't see that blue uniform anywhere in the crowd, and I didn't feel like asking anyone. Then I had an idea. A cab was what I was after. I'd get the cabbie to take me to a police station, and the police could find Miss Lillingsworth and SP, and tell the Professor, and… My plan didn't go any further than that.

Now I could see a line of hansom cabs waiting for

fares. I felt sorry for the horses, working so late on a cold night, but at least the two-wheeled cabs weren't heavy to pull. I went up to the first one in the line.

"I haven't any money…" I began.

"You don't get no ride, then," the cabbie said, and turned his back to me.

I tried the next one. "My friends will see to it that you get paid when…"

"I drive for a fare, not for a promise."

Well, it was clear now I was going the wrong way about it. I approached the next cabbie differently.

"I'd like to go to the nearest police station, please," I said.

But the first cabbie yelled down the line, "Don't you listen to 'er, Sam. She ain't got no money."

Sam growled at me. "Off you go. And don't hang around here, botherin' the punters."

"But how am I going to get to the—"

"Same as everyone without a fare. You walk."

I walked to the corner and then stopped. I didn't even know where I was going.

"Get out of the way," someone said, bumping me sideways.

"Move along," said another, and I found myself swept along with the stream of people, buffeted and trodden on, through the brightly lit streets. At last

I pushed and shoved my way out of the crowd, and slipped around a corner. There I leaned, trembling, against the side of a haberdashery shop.

I felt like I couldn't go on. I was tired and aching all over; I was worried sick about SP and Miss Lillingsworth; and worse still, I was right at the very end of my courage. My mind went back to Ma. If she was here, watching over me, what would she want me to do?

I don't know why I looked across the street just then. What I saw was a lighted shop with the sign of the three balls on it. Underneath that was written in large gold letters:

Vassily Plotkin
Money Lent Upon Every Description
of Valuable Property

A pawnbroker. My hand went to the red cord around my neck. Ma's ring was gold. It must be worth a dozen cab fares. What would Ma want me to do? All at once I knew. She'd want me to pawn her ring and help SP and Miss Lillingsworth.

A bell tinkled as I opened the door. At the back of the shop an elderly bearded man sat surrounded by furniture and racks of clothes and cases of jewellery and trinkets, and telescopes and stuffed birds under glass and brass trumpets and I can't say what else, but the shop was very clean and neat all the same. He had a coffee pot on a burner. The familiar comforting smell made me think of home. Mulberry Hill. How I longed to be back there, safe and sound, with this nightmare over. I was close to tears.

"What can I do for you, little miss?" The man had a very deep voice, slightly foreign.

I held out the ring. "Can I have ... can I have some money for it, please, sir?"

He peered over his wire-rimmed specs. "You have fallen over?"

"Yes, sir."

He looked me up and down, taking in my new boots and my fine wool dress. I could tell he was wondering why I was here in his shop, covered in mud and trying to pawn a ring.

"The ring was my mother's," I said. I didn't want him to think I'd stolen it.

He took it from me and inspected it closely. "It is a Russian wedding ring. See, there are three kinds of gold – rose, yellow and white. It is a lovely thing. Why do you pawn it, little miss?"

"I need money for a cab," I said. "I don't know what happened to our coachman, but someone else

was driving, and he attacked my friend, and…"
I started to tremble.

"Sit down, little miss." He put a cup of coffee into
my hand.

"And I ran and ran and he chased me and there
were these men and…"

"Eat this." It was a sweet roll.

"And I'm lost, and the cabbie wouldn't take me
without the fare. Please, sir, I don't know what to
do."

"Let me think about your problem while you finish
your coffee and your roll," he said. He seemed very
kind and I now felt quite safe with him in the circle
of lamplight. He asked me who my friends were,
and where they lived, and wrinkled his brows as he
thought and thought. "Now, this is what I will do. I will
go with you to the police station, and after that, I will
send you home. I will pay for the cab, and you can keep
the lovely ring that was your mother's. It will be a loan
with no security, but I think that I can trust you."

"You can, you can." I took his hand. "Thank you
so much, sir."

He nodded and looked at me with his gentle
brown eyes. "You will come back and see me, no?
And repay your loan?"

"Yes, of course."

Mr Plotkin closed up the shop. We found a cab, and I started to thank him again, but he shook his head. "What were we put on earth for, if not to help one another? Do not worry. You know, I predict that in no time at all, you will be home safe with your friends."

15

DEAD ENDS AND CLUES

To tell the truth, I had my doubts, but Mr Plotkin was right after all.

"Thank goodness, miss," one of the policemen said, after we walked in to the police station and I started to tell my story. "We've had five men out searching for you. Mr Plush is well known to the constabulary – I mean that in a good way – and as soon as we heard, we were onto it."

"Inspector Grade is handling the case," said another. "We're to take you to your friends' house, not keep you here, you being a young lady and all." He looked me up and down. "You look dead beat, miss, and no wonder, running all that way. Since the cab's still waiting, we'll just pop you back in and Constable Griggs'll go with you. And Mr Plotkin, I'll find a cab for you, sir. A regular good Samaritan you've been tonight. We'll have her back with her friends in two shakes of a lamb's tail."

It took a little longer than that, but by midnight Constable Griggs had delivered me to Miss Lillingsworth's, and she had me clutched to her chest like she'd never let go.

"I'm all right, Miss Lillingsworth," I said. "I've had a few adventures, but I'm right as rain, truly I am."

When at last she believed me, she told me that she'd had a few adventures of her own. After the man ran off after me, she revived poor SP and helped him back into the carriage. As soon as she changed her calls of "Help!" to "Fire!", a nightwatchman ran to her aid. He got the police, and the police got them home and sent word to the Professor. Then all she had to worry about was SP's head and finding me.

"Miss Lillingsworth," I said. "What a terrible time you've had."

"Nonsense. I've been through worse, my dear — why, when I was teaching the Lampedusa children in Sicily, we were captured by bandits. No, the only terrible thing was the worry about you and SP."

Miss Lillingsworth, I thought, was made of very tough stuff.

"Is SP badly hurt?" I asked.

"He got a nasty blow to the head, and the doctor's with him now in the parlour," she said. "I must get back to him. Millie will look after you, won't you, Millie?"

Millie actually gave me a hug, and then she bustled me downstairs to the kitchen, where she bandaged my grazed hands, sponged the mud off my skirt and gave me a cup of hot cocoa and some buttered toast.

"Finish your supper, and don't you fret about your friend, miss," she said, seeing I was a mite twitchy and anxious to get upstairs. "He's got Sir Barrington Topp with him, and as he's the personal physician to the Duke of Cambridge, he ought to be good enough for Mr Saddington Plush."

Eventually, she let me go into the front parlour where SP was lying on the sofa with cold compresses on his forehead. It seemed he was asleep.

Sir Barrington, looking like a toff in his evening suit and smelling of gardenias, was just about to leave.

"The young man has sustained a blow. The brain naturally resents being thrown around inside the skull and, as any injured tissue is liable to do, it swells," he was saying. Even though he was trying to whisper, his voice was loud and plummy, and it was clear he liked the sound of it. "Our patient needs to be kept quite quiet, in a darkened room, on a bland diet, for at least a week. I have prescribed a sedative and a sleeping draught." He scanned the room, as if half expecting applause, and then his eye lit on me. "So this is our young friend. Another patient for me, Maria?" In spite of my saying I was perfectly fine, he insisted on taking my pulse, looking at my tongue and feeling my forehead before he was satisfied.

"My work is done," he said, and with that he gathered up his top hat, cloak and cane, and said, in quite a different tone, "Good night, Maria dear, and let me know if you need me again, won't you?"

"Yes, Barry, I will. Thank you for coming."

"Any time," he said, and kissed her on the cheek.

Miss Lillingsworth watched him leave the room. "He's so good to his old governess," she said fondly. "He was such a shy little boy too. He's come out of himself wonderfully. Now, Saddington." She tapped him gently on the shoulder. "Here is Verity, as I told you, quite safe." She turned to me and whispered, "He's been in agonies of worry about you."

SP spoke like he was still dreaming. "It's really you, Verity?"

"It is, SP, and I'm safe and sound so there's no need to worry yourself."

"Really, Verity?" SP sounded weak as a kitten.

"Really," I said, kneeling next to him. "A few scrapes, but no harm done."

"Tell ... tell Inspector Grade..."

185

For the first time I noticed someone sitting in the shadows near the fireplace. He was a small balding man, wearing a baggy tweed suit. He stood up and offered his hand, and I noticed that under his bristly ginger moustache he had bad teeth and a very kind smile.

"I'm Inspector Grade, and I'm glad to see you, miss," he said. "And I'm very glad you're unharmed. A nasty thing for a young lady like yourself to be running at night through those streets. But here you are, and that's one less of Her Majesty's subjects in harm's way, for which I'm grateful. Are you up to giving me a statement?" He flipped the pages of his notebook.

"Statement?"

"If you'll just tell me what happened, that'll be good enough for Her Majesty."

There wasn't really much to tell. All I could say for certain was that the man who chased me was tall and well-spoken.

"And his voice was quite unusual."

"Can you elaborate on that?"

"Very deep and sort of smooth, if you know what I mean. He had a way of talking that wasn't foreign, like Mr Savinov or Mr Plotkin, but somehow different. Like a gentleman, but ... but not quite."

Inspector Grade's pen was poised in mid-air. But I just couldn't put my finger on it.

"He was a good runner too," I said, trying to be helpful.

"Could be a young man. Could be an active older man."

"Young, I think, sir." But when he asked me why I thought that, I couldn't tell him. Dookie, Sam, Polly and the rest of the urchins might have had a better look at him, but I didn't want to send the police round to Flash Harry's, for they'd move them on, or worse – round them up and put them in some poorhouse where they'd be separated. It was no way to thank them, so I said nothing.

I was giving Inspector Grade more useless answers when the knocker banged loudly. We heard voices and footsteps in the hall, and Mr Opie burst into the room.

"SP, old chap."

"Shhh," said Miss Lillingsworth.

"Sorry, Maria," he said, in a hoarse whisper. "SP, I was with the Professor when the message came. I just had to let you know. We found John. He was in the mews behind Lady Skewe's house, wrists and ankles tied with rope, and doped with chloroform."

"Is he all right?" asked SP.

"A thumping headache, but no worse than that, thank God. He says that he was having a stroll when a cloth was put over his face. He saw no one, and heard nothing."

"Chloroform, eh?" said Inspector Grade. "Then it was all well planned and executed. Not a robbery, that's plain. What was he after?" He chewed the end of his pencil and then looked at me sharply. "The answer seems to be you, miss, seeing as how he ran in pursuit. He called your name too. Anything else unusual happened to you recently? Anything at all?"

"I had a letter," I said. "A letter warning me away from the Plushes."

"Do you still have it?" asked the inspector.

"No, I threw it in the rubbish."

"Pity. Anything else?"

"I had a note from a friend, asking me to meet her. She wasn't there, and when I saw her later, she knew nothing about it."

"You mean she didn't write to you at all? Aha." He scribbled busily. "So what's the motive?" Inspector Grade went on, half to himself.

I started to tell the inspector about Lady Throttle, Miss Charlotte and Mic-Mac Pinner, but Mr Opie interrupted.

"They're almost certainly out of the picture,

Verity. Mic-Mac is in gaol, and Miss Charlotte has run off with the strongman from Leopoldi's Circus. She'd be in Brussels by now. Without them, Lady Throttle has no accomplices. And more importantly, she has no money."

SP groaned. Then he groaned again, louder.

"I think our patient has had enough now, Inspector," said Miss Lillingsworth.

SP nodded slowly and said, "Thank you, Inspector," in a thread of a voice.

"It's simply my duty, sir; I do my best for Her Majesty." He snapped his notebook shut. "But I will need to speak to you again, sir." He turned to me. "And you too, miss. Will you be staying here, or—"

"I will give you the Plushes' address on your way out," said Miss Lillingsworth, and she practically chased him out of the room.

SP sat up so abruptly that the cold compress went flying. "Verity," he said. "This can't go on. You're in danger; perhaps we're all in danger, and we won't know why until we've solved this mystery."

"I agree," said Mr Opie. "We mustn't delay."

"What mystery?" I asked, looking from one to the other.

SP answered. *The truth about Verity Sparks.*

The truth about Verity Sparks! Finding it was

going to be easier said than done, for we had only scraps and shadows to go on. Somewhere, if Miss Lillingsworth was right about the lucky piece, I had six aunts and six sisters, maybe even a mother still alive. I could be French, but if so, why was I left with the Sparkses of Seacoal Lane? Where did the Russian wedding ring fit in? And what was the meaning of *la Belle Sauvage*?

But SP was right. I had to find out who I was. Someone was after me, and next time I might not be so lucky.

16

LA BELLE SAUVAGE AND
AUNTIE SARAH

There was quite a hullabaloo when we got back at last to Mulberry Hill the following afternoon. The Professor, with a red nose and a cough, in his nightcap and dressing-gown; Mrs Cannister, Etty, Cook and Sarah, all wide-eyed and curious; Judith, pale and worried; Amy, silly and excited – all of them were waiting in the hall as the carriage drew up outside the door.

"My dear boy," whispered the Professor.

"Oh, SP," cried Judith.

SP smiled, and then wobbled. Before Mr Opie and I could catch him, he slumped to the floor in a dead faint.

It was the Professor and Mr Opie who got stuck into the case, for after the blow to the head, poor SP was sick with headaches and dizzy spells and fainting fits, and so, much against his will, he had to obey Sir Barrington's orders about bed and a darkened room.

"Here is my plan of action," said the Professor, unfolding a large sheet of paper covered in writing and circles and lines and arrows. "Our first clue is the lucky piece, and Miss Lillingsworth is onto that. She's finding out everything she can about the *septième étoile*. She's already written to one of her old students in Paris in the hope that he can dig up a little information for us, and she's asking all of her spiritualist friends. Our second clue is the ring." He took it out of his waistcoat pocket and handed it back to me.

The Professor had been quite excited when I first showed it to him, and had insisted that I try to "read" it then and there. But I had nothing from it, except a kind of rustling sound that sounded like stiff satin skirts, so he'd taken it off to be looked at by both Miss Lillingsworth and his friend Mr Osprey, the famous Bond Street jeweller. "It's a bit disappointing. Neither psychometry or the jeweller's eye has been able to tell anything other than it was a wedding ring, and it was made in Paris. The Russian style, Mr Osprey said, is quite in vogue with the Continentals."

"What about *la Belle Sauvage?*" suggested Mr Opie.

"Yes, I've written that here," said the Professor.

He stabbed at the scribbly page with his pen. "Opie, perhaps you could take Verity there tomorrow. And there's your Aunt Sarah, Verity. She must know something. There are no other relatives?"

"Not that I know of."

"Well, we have two paths to follow," said Mr Opie. "*La Belle Sauvage* and Aunt Sarah. That's a start."

La Belle Sauvage. I'd had such hopes, and what a washout that was. When Mr Opie and I got to Seacoal Lane, there was nothing there. There were a few warehouses, a dingy teashop and a printer's, but the little lane had been eaten up by the Chatham and Eastern Metropolitan Line and a monstrous great viaduct loomed over everything. The ground shook as trains trundled overhead, spreading noise, soot and smoke. One of the printer's men told us that the inn had been demolished five years ago.

"Do you remember anything about the inn?" Mr Opie asked me.

"We moved away when I was three."

I couldn't even remember what number we'd lived at. I didn't recognize anything. I'd hoped there might be a shoemaker's there still, and a residence upstairs. I'd imagined being invited up to see the rooms, and a kind old lady giving me something she'd found all those years ago, under a loose floorboard maybe, or tucked away on a high shelf. A letter, a locket, some lawyer's papers. Something – anything – that would lead me to the truth. It was the kind of thing that happened in the stories Cook read to us, but it wasn't going to happen to me.

"*La Belle Sauvage* turned out to be a dead end, eh, Verity?" said Mr Opie.

I shrugged. "The message must have been for Madame Dumas after all."

When we got back to Mulberry Hill, Judith was waiting for us. We hadn't time to catch our breath before she started in on Mr Opie.

"Where have you been? You've been gone for hours. Poor SP was worried sick."

Mr Opie was unprepared. "Miss Judith," he said. "I'm sorry I didn't inform you. Or SP. But ... but the Professor knew where we were."

"He went out."

"I'm sorry, Miss Judith, I didn't think—"

"Think. Think. What's the use of expecting you men to think." She was well and truly worked up by now, but I couldn't for the life of me work out why. Her face was red and angry and I couldn't help staring.

"And another thing," she continued. "Not one of

you has bothered telling me what this investigation is about. You have left me out completely, as if I was no help at all."

Mr Opie goggled at her, lost for words, and she started on another tack. "And I should think you'd have the sense to see that Verity needs a female along on these madcap expeditions. She needs someone to look after her."

Which was silly, 'cos I'd been trotting around London on my own since I was ten. And I'll tell you this for free: I could have looked after her better than she could've looked after me.

"I'm sorry, Miss Judith. I'd be happy to explain the investigation to you. And if you wish to come along tomorrow..."

"Tomorrow? What's happening tomorrow?"

"The Professor asked me to contact Verity's aunt. I did so, and we are going to meet her tomorrow morning."

At first Auntie Sarah had said no, but Mr Opie laid it on thick about me wanting to see her, and she finally agreed to meet us in old St Ethelbald's churchyard at half past ten.

"Then I shall come with you," Judith said in a determined voice.

"Thank you, Miss Judith. That will be a great help."

She stared at him for a few seconds, as if she suspected he was teasing her.

"Very well, then, Mr Opie. Till tomorrow." She held out her hand, and I noticed that he held it for rather longer than was necessary.

St Ethelbald's, a tiny church tucked into a dead-end lane not far from Liverpool Street Station, was a dismal place. The whole right side was propped up with scaffolding and timbers, weeds grew on the roof, and the whole building was crumbling away with damp and time. The churchyard was at the side. In it, the gravestones stood as close together as workers on a cheap-fare train. The surrounding buildings must have gobbled up some of the burying ground, for a red brick wall cut off one corner, and against it headstones were stacked neatly like playing cards. In the other corner, broken slabs with bits of lettering and angels' heads and carved skulls on them were all jumbled together in a pile, with a tree growing out of the middle. There was a lone figure under it. It was Auntie Sarah. She came forward a few steps and then stopped.

"Good morning, Mrs Bird," said Mr Opie. "Thank you for—"

"Who is she?" interrupted Auntie Sarah in a whisper, pointing at Judith.

"This is Miss Plush," said Mr Opie. "Verity works for Miss Plush's father."

"Much obliged to you, ma'am, and I hope she gives satisfaction," said Auntie Sarah in a rush, and then stood silently, trembling. I could tell Mr Opie made her nervous. And so could he.

"We will wait for you under the porch, Verity," he said, and taking Judith by the arm, they moved away out of earshot. Auntie Sarah pulled her shawl around her. She was thinner than I remembered.

"No one knows I'm here," she said, as if to reassure herself. "Bill's gone to Gravesend and he won't be back till the afternoon. But be quick, Verity. I haven't much time. You're all right, aren't you? The gent said you weren't at the hat shop any more; he said you were working for some professor. That's Miss Plush's father, is it?"

"Yes, Auntie."

"And they treat you right, do they?"

"They treat me very well. Like one of the family."

Her eyes widened, and then she nodded, talking half to herself, as if something was worrying her. "Then all's well. Lizzie, I said, I don't know how I can have 'er, with Bill the way he is … but you've got a job, and they're good to you?"

"Yes, they are."

197

"Well, that's a weight off me mind. Is that all?" She glanced nervously around her.

"Please ... I need to know who Ma got me from."

"What do you mean?" Her eyes narrowed. "Did Bill say something to you? What did he tell you?"

"That I was a foundling. That Ma found me in a basket on the doorstep."

She bit her lip. "He was never supposed to tell you that. But then I was never supposed to tell him, was I? Except he's got a way of weaselling things out of a person." She shivered. "It's true. But you were never left in a basket like no one wanted you – what nonsense. It was someone that she knew from her days at the opera gave you to Lizzie."

"The opera?"

"Lizzie made costumes for the Theatre Royal in Covent Garden – did she never tell you? It was one of the theatre people that brought you to her in Seacoal Lane. Now, what was his name? A dresser, I think he was; that's like a valet. Victor. That's right, Victor Drummond."

Victor Drummond. A dresser at the Theatre Royal... All sorts of ideas and possibilities started tumbling around in my brain. He was my father, and his wife had died. Or he'd got a girl into trouble. Or he was my uncle, or my grandfather, or...

"What was he to me? Why did he give me to Ma?"

"I don't know, Lizzie never said." Her eyes were wet. "She was a good woman, Lizzie. A good woman."

"I know, Auntie."

"She was the best of sisters. And Thomas, your Pa … he was a good man too. They were happy."

"I know."

She was quiet for a few seconds, but then she started looking around her nervously again. "I have to go, Verity. I'm not meant to go out, and if he comes back early and finds me gone…"

"Don't go back to him," I said on impulse.

"Don't go back to him? How could I leave? I haven't got any money; I haven't got anywhere to go." She touched her face like she was feeling an old bruise. "He'd be after me, anyway. It's too late, don't you see? I've made my bed, and I must lie in it."

I put my hand on her arm, but she eased it off.

"Goodbye, Verity," she said. She turned and ran past the dripping gravestones, through the iron gates and out into the street. I started to run after her, but Mr Opie caught me by the arm.

"Let her go," he said.

Judith patted me awkwardly. "Shall we have some tea?"

Tea. For once it was welcome.

17

MISS MINNIE LOVE AND HER INCOMPARABLE ALBUMS

That night I kept thinking about the tombstones. No longer marking their graves, but just stacked in piles along the churchyard wall with the lettering mossy and crumbling away, names forgotten. And yet they'd all been somebody's children. Maybe even mothers or fathers as well.

I'd been to Ma and Pa's grave only once. Auntie Sarah took me when Uncle Bill was away. It was in Brookwood cemetery; that's where all the East Enders are buried, and we went there by the London Necropolis train. It looked like the gravestones rolled on and on to the world's end. Auntie told me it was the biggest cemetery in the world. I was only nine, and it didn't seem quite real to me then. I remember worrying about Ma and Pa being there in the ground with so many strangers.

I tossed and turned, and in the end I got up. I lit the candle and opened the top drawer of my chest. I'd tried the ring and I'd tried the lucky piece. What about the little quilt? It was Ma's handiwork and if I could read anything, surely it would be this. Breathing slow and steady like Miss Lillingsworth said, I took it out and spread it on my lap.

I concentrated. Miss Lillingsworth had told me she imagined she was in a mist, and I tried that, but my mind just ran on foggy London days with wet feet and traffic accidents. I tried to see a clear blue sky, but how often d'you get one of those? I tried to see nothing at all.

I was about to give up, when my fingers tingled, just like before.

Thread. That's what I saw. White thread and a silver needle. A pair of hands, working quickly, pecking like little birds at the patterned silk. That was all.

"Ma?"

The sound of my own voice broke the spell. Ma was dead, and this was all wrong. Let her be, I thought. I crumpled the quilt into the drawer and blew out the candle. I was no nearer to the truth than before.

Mr Opie – or Daniel as I now called him – had

contacts everywhere, and he found someone who could help us. Mr Octavius Orchid, a stage manager at the Theatre Royal, suggested we visit an elderly lady called Miss Minnie Love. She'd worked as a fitter in the theatre's costume workshops until about ten years ago, and knew all the workers and performers. And what was more, she had scrapbooks of clippings relating to the theatre that went back thirty years.

"D'you want to come with us, Miss Judith?" Daniel asked with a twinkle in his eye, but she didn't twinkle back. She'd had a call from Mr Tissot the day before. Kathleen was ill, and she was going to sit with her.

"Is it as we thought?" asked Daniel, suddenly serious.

Judith nodded. I looked from one to the other. "What's wrong?" I asked.

"Consumption," said Judith.

"Oh." A shadow fell on the day. Consumption – tuberculosis, doctors called it – was as good as a death sentence. Consumptives could try all sorts of cures – quacks and faith healers and rest homes and spas – but they got paler and thinner and coughed up blood, and in the end they faded away and died. There was nothing anyone could do about it. Poor Kathleen, so pretty and bright. Poor Mr Tissot.

Daniel squeezed Judith's hand as we left the

house. "Give her my love," he said, but he was looking straight into Judith's eyes.

Miss Minnie Love lived in a theatrical boarding house in the shabby end of Golden Square. We opened the front door into a narrow hallway that smelt of cabbage, and were stopped from going further by a big, tall woman who swung out from one of the side doors. She stood with her arms crossed in front of the staircase, blocking our way.

"Mrs Costello?" asked Daniel.

"That is my name. How may I help you?" Her voice was ever so genteel, but her face, all shiny and mottled, looked like a common pork sausage.

"We've come to see Miss Love," said Daniel, drawing back slightly. Mrs Costello reeked of sweat and beer.

She stood there for a few seconds, as if thinking hard. Then she yelled, so loudly it made us both jump, "Ivy!"

A maidservant with a greasy apron and smuts all over her face darted out from the other side door. "Ma'am?"

"Pray, show these visitors up to Miss Minnie." She turned and slammed the door behind her.

"This way, sir, miss," said Ivy.

She went to lead the way, but Daniel said, "Just tell us. I'm sure we can find it."

"Thank you, sir," she said. "I'm that busy."

And tired and put-upon and underfed, I thought. Daniel slipped her a coin as he passed, and I hoped that Mrs Costello didn't take it off her.

The stairs were so steep they were the next thing to a ladder. The cabbage smell and the sound of someone practising scales on the violin followed us up into the hallway. There were five attic rooms, and Miss Minnie's was the last. Daniel knocked softly.

"Who's there?" The voice was barely a whisper.

"My name is Daniel Opie. Mr Orchid suggested I call on you. He said you may be able to help me with some inquiries about the opera."

"The opera!" We heard mouse-like scrabblings from behind the door, and then it opened a crack. Two bright eyes peeped out. "You want to find out about the opera?"

"Indeed, Miss Love, if you have the time. Mr Orchid says that your scrapbooks are incomparable. Here is my card." A tiny hand flashed out and snatched it. The door shut again for a few seconds, and then opened wide.

Miss Minnie Love looked like a little girl – a wizened, elderly little girl with grey hair hanging in loose ringlets down to her shoulders and a dress like a frilled lampshade. It was hard not to stare, because it was more than twenty years since that had been the mode.

Waving her hand like a duchess, she said, "Mr Opie, won't you come in? And Miss ... Miss?"

"Forgive me, Miss Love," said Daniel, bowing. "Allow me to present my friend, Miss Verity Sparks."

I bobbed a curtsey, and she held out her hand, smiling. It was like holding a dead sparrow, limp and light and barely there.

"Tea?"

We refused, just to be polite, but she insisted. She lit a spirit lamp to boil the kettle and even brought out a box of fancy biscuits to go with our very weak brew. "They're a present from Mr Orchid," she said. "He knows cherry macaroons are my weakness."

She whisked a quilt and pillows off the sofa and gestured to us to sit. I looked around the room. The walls were papered with posters and playbills and pictures cut from the newspapers. Every other surface was covered. She had sprays of artificial flowers and framed pictures, piles of velvet and tumbles of gold braid, three hatstands with fancy hats on them, a stuffed peacock, a statue of a naked lady, and books. Stacks and stacks of books. They were atlases and albums and illustrated guides and goodness knows what, swelled to two or three times their natural size and fanned open from the clippings pasted inside. I imagined the hours and hours she must she have spent on them.

"Yes," she said, seeing my wide eyes. "They are incomparable, Mr Orchid says. Mr Orchid is most kind. But I think he may be right, you know." She murmured something that Daniel told me later was French and Italian. "*Thursa... Les Belles Fromagieres... Il Gattopardo di Palermo...*" She stroked her scrapbooks as if they were pets.

"Now, Mr Opie, what is it that you wish to know?" she said, all of a sudden quite businesslike.

"We are seeking information about two different parties, Miss Love. The first is Lizzie Hughes; Lizzie Sparks was her married name. She was the adoptive mother of Miss Sparks here."

"Lizzie?" Miss Love's hands ran like spiders over the covers of her scrapbooks. "Yes, yes, I remember her. She was one of our costumiers. She sewed all the costumes for the ballet in *La Princesse de Russie*. Beautiful they were, all white velvet and fur."

I remembered the day I dozed off outside Mr and Mrs Rhodes's house in Carisbrook Grove. I dreamed Ma had been sewing white velvet and fur. Only it wasn't a dream.

206

"Do you remember anything about her?" I asked eagerly.

Miss Minnie thought for a few seconds. "She was a good worker. Quiet. Her stitching was even and neat, as if done by machine."

I was disappointed. Was Ma nothing but neat stitches and good, quiet work?

"Is that all?" I asked.

"I think so." She put her head to one side like a little bird. "Lizzie ... Lizzie Sparks. There was something..." But she couldn't remember. "And the other party?"

"The other party is a man, a dresser called Victor Drummond. He worked at the opera about thirteen years ago."

Miss Minnie frowned, and her fingers all on their own started reaching towards her towers of books. She fingered them until she found the right one, and she slipped it onto her knee. "1865," she muttered to herself. "Who was there that season? Signor Boldini, Signor Bandelli..." She gazed into nothingness, face lit up by memories, and her lips moved silently. Then she said in a decided tone, "You are not looking for a man at all."

I didn't understand. "I beg your pardon?"

"It is Victoire Drummond you seek. A woman. Mrs Vic, we called her."

The sudden tingling in my fingers was so sharp that I gasped out loud. I stared at my hands. Were they telling me I was close to knowing who my mother was?

"Here we are," said Miss Minnie dramatically as she opened the book and put her finger on a newspaper cutting. It was not about the opera, however.

TRAGEDY STRIKES TWICE AT PRIMA DONNA'S MANSION

The musical world is still reeling from the tragic fire that took the life of prima donna Isabella Savage and her infant daughter. But now tragedy strikes again in the death of Madame Savage's devoted dresser and personal maid, Mrs Victoire Drummond. Only a week after the fire, Mrs Drummond accidentally plunged to her death down two flights of stairs, breaking her spine.

Before I had time to feel too cast down by the fact that Victoire Drummond was dead, Miss Minnie flipped to another book and opened at a page from the *Weekly Sketch*. It showed a pretty dark-haired woman in some kind of fancy dress with two maids fussing around her and a woman in black standing alongside. The line underneath said:

Prima Donna Madame Savage prepares for her performance in Les Orphelines de Marseilles.

Pointing at the woman in black, Miss Love said, "That's she. That's Mrs Vic."

"Are you sure?" I squinted at the yellowed picture.

"Oh, yes."

"That's Mrs Vic?"

"Of course it is. I know everything about the opera," Miss Minnie said, quite without vanity.

Victoire Drummond was an old lady, and she couldn't possibly have been my mother. So who was? Questions and more questions, possibilities and more possibilities. Did Mrs Vic have children – a daughter perhaps, whose child she took to Seacoal Lane? Or maybe she was close to one of the other costumiers or performers. Who was the desperate young woman who entrusted her baby daughter to Mrs Vic?

"Look, Verity," said Daniel, pointing. The line above the picture, in bold black letters, read:

LA BELLE SAUVAGE IN LONDON DEBUT

Prima Donna Madame Isabella Savage, also known as la Belle Sauvage...

"La Belle Sauvage." I turned to Daniel. "It isn't a place, it's a person."

18

CASE CLOSED

We got home to find that the Professor had to consult on a case, and was staying for a couple of nights in town at the Megatherium Club. Judith was still with the Tissots, and SP was propped up on a couch in the small downstairs sitting room. He was half asleep when Daniel and I burst in to tell him of our discoveries, but he was soon sitting up straight and scribbling notes in one of his leather-bound casebooks.

"At least we've another lead," he said. "Victoire Drummond. Victoire is a French name, and I wonder if there's a connection with the *septième étoile*."

"And there's *la Belle Sauvage*," I added. "Mr Egg told us it was the name of an old inn in Seacoal Lane where I used to live, but it's the name of an opera singer as well. Isabella Savage was known as *la Belle Sauvage*."

"Can we find out more about her?"

"We're going to visit Miss Love again on Friday," I said. "She's going to consult her albums and make us a list of all the people who would have worked at the opera with Isabella Savage and Mrs Vic. And she's going to see if she can remember anything more about Ma."

"It seems as if we are making progress at last," said SP. "Just as well I'm over this blasted concussion at last." He swung his legs off the sofa and stood up. "And this time I can come too."

When Judith got back from visiting Kathleen, it turned out she didn't want to be left out either, so there was a party of four to visit Miss Love. She was expecting us to call at two o'clock on Friday, but we left early, for I'd asked if we could call in to Mr Plotkin's shop. I would have hated him to think I'd forgotten his kindness. Or that I still owed him the cab fare.

At first Mr Plotkin didn't recognize me, for I was not the bedraggled girl who'd come into his shop that night a week ago. But then he looked again.

"Little miss," he said. "How good it is to see you again." Behind his wire-rimmed specs he was taking in every detail. "You are well?"

"I am very well, Mr Plotkin," I said.

"Thanks to God." He took both my hands in his. "It is good that you are safe now, and with your friends." He glanced sideways at SP and Judith, and SP stepped forwards.

"Mr Plotkin, please allow me to introduce myself," he said, holding out his hand. "I am Saddington Plush, and this is my sister, Miss Judith Plush. We are most grateful to you, sir, for helping Verity on that terrible night."

"Are you, sir, the gentleman who was attacked? But no bones broken, I see."

"No damage done," said SP heartily. No bones, that was true, but whatever he said to the contrary, Miss Judith and I both knew that he wasn't quite over the concussion.

"We'd like very much to repay you," said Judith. "Verity told us that you generously paid for her cab fare home."

"The little one was in trouble, Miss Plush," he said. "What else should I do?"

She opened her purse and took out a coin. "Here, Mr Plotkin, with our thanks."

"No, no, no." He took a step backwards. "The cab fare was not even a quarter that, Miss Plush. I have no need of a reward."

"But I insist."

"So do I. Please do not insult me." He really looked distressed, and SP quickly changed the subject.

"You have some wonderful things here," SP said. "These for instance." He pointed to a glass case. In it was a flight of tiny butterflies the colour of peacock silk, set on black velvet like jewels. "How perfect they are," said SP.

"Wouldn't Aunt Almeria love them?" said Judith. "They're from Northern Queensland – in Australia, SP. Let's get it for her as a surprise for when she gets over her snit and comes home."

Smiling, Mr Plotkin named a price. The butterfly in its case was wrapped up in tissue paper and then brown paper, and with lots more smiles Mr Plotkin saw us out of the shop.

Our carriage was waiting for us around the corner. We'd only gone a few steps when SP swayed slightly and sank to the pavement.

"I told you it was too soon to come out, but you wouldn't listen," scolded Judith.

"Oh, Judith, always the pessimist," he said. "I am perfectly well." He struggled to his feet between the two of us and then his knees gave way again.

"Let's take him back into Mr Plotkin's shop," I said. "I'll go and get John to come with the carriage so he doesn't have to walk."

Mr Plotkin calmly shifted a stuffed owl off a sofa, and sat SP down with his legs up and a small glass of brandy in his hand.

"No trouble, no trouble at all," he kept insisting. "It is good for an old man to feel he is of some use."

When SP had a bit of colour back in his cheeks, I set off around the corner. I could see our carriage, with John up in the box reading the sporting news, a little way down. First, I had to pass by another carriage. A tall man wrapped up in an overcoat and with a scarf half covering his face was waiting next to it, and I expected him to move sideways to let me pass. But he blocked my way. I had a prickling feeling all along my spine that something wasn't right, and then I looked up at his face. Those eyes, so fishy and cold. I recognized them at once.

"You!"

He grabbed me by the arm. "Miss Sparks, you're coming with me."

I tried to shake him off, but he wouldn't let go.

"Come on!" He attempted to force me towards the carriage, so I stamped on his foot and then punched him on the nose. He just stood there, so surprised it was almost comic, and then he fell to his knees in the gutter, holding his face and moaning. I would have laughed if I hadn't been busy yelling for John to go and get a constable.

John ran off up to the main street, and all of a sudden there was someone else beside me on the footpath. I glanced up. It was a tall, handsome, fair-haired gentleman. It crossed my mind that he seemed vaguely familiar.

"May I help?" he said. "It appears this man is bothering you."

"He certainly is," I said, and at that my would-be kidnapper glared at me.

"Bothering?" he said. "Bothering? Why, this little she-devil has just broken my nose."

Who was he to call me a she-devil? I'm afraid I really lost my temper then. They say you shouldn't kick a man when he's down, but I did. Hard.

"And you, Dr Beale, are no gentleman," I said.

Quick as a wink, John was back with a member of the Metropolitan Police.

"What's this then?" the constable asked sternly. "Robbery? Assault?"

"Assault!" cried Dr Beale. He was practically frothing at the mouth by now, what with being punched in the nose by a mere girl and then held with his arms behind his back by a tall and very strong

216

gentleman. Not to mention being sworn at by John. "I'm the one who's been assaulted."

"Or is it kidnapping?" asked the constable.

"Of course it wasn't kidnapping. I'd offered her fifty pounds for a week and the unreasonable chit refused. After all, my sister would have been there."

The constable was unimpressed. "Well, sir," he said, grasping Dr Beale by the arm. "I think you'd better come along with me."

We went to Mr Plotkin's shop first.

"Dr Beale," said SP with a puzzled look on his face. Then he noticed the constable, and the puzzlement increased. "What on earth ... and Alex!"

The handsome blond gentleman grinned. "Hello, SP."

"What are you doing here?"

"Rescuing your young friend," he said. "How are you, Plush, old chap?"

"What an amazing coincidence," said SP. "Verity Sparks, this is Alexander, Mr Savinov's son."

"How do you do, Miss Sparks." Alexander gave a little bow from the waist. I thought I'd seen him somewhere before – and I had. In Mr Tissot's portrait.

"A complete misunderstanding."

That's what Dr Beale kept saying on the way to

the Market Street police station. But SP had already told the constable the story of Dr Beale's offer and my refusal, followed by the letters and then the frightening incident the night of the seance, and the constable had drawn his own conclusions.

"You still need to come and answer some questions, sir."

"But it was purely an accidental meeting," he insisted. "I simply offered to escort Miss Sparks back to her friends, and she hit me. For no reason. I demand that you let me go this instant."

"No demanding, thank you, sir. Just you come along with me, and we'll sort this out."

"There's nothing to sort out." Dr Beale raised his voice. "I'll have you know that I'm a doctor!"

But the constable had had enough of his malarkey. "Then you ought to know better," he said, and marched Dr Beale up the steps of the police station. A uniformed man sat in a kind of dock at the entrance. He looked up from his ledger as we crowded in.

"What's this?" he said.

"One for the cells," said the constable, and then muttered, "Or maybe the loony bin."

"What's going on?" said another voice, and into the waiting hall came Inspector Grade. His eyes widened when he saw our lot.

"Gentleman, the name of Dr Beale, attempting abduction, broad daylight," said the constable, standing to attention and rattling out the information like a kettledrum. "Known to victim. Possible history of harassing victim by poison-pen letters."

"Absolute rubbish!" Dr Beale shouted. He tried to struggle out of the constable's grip.

"Possible stalking victim. Possible other attempts——"

"I demand that you let me go." Dr Beale was working himself up into a frenzy. "I demand to see the Chief of Police! I demand to see the Home Secretary!"

I thought he was going to try to make a run for it, but when the constable produced his truncheon, Dr Beale abruptly sagged like a puppet with the strings gone slack. Even though he'd caused me such grief, I felt a little sorry for him then.

"I'll take this one, constable," said Inspector Grade. "Her Majesty will be highly gratified that this case is finally solved. And I have to say, I'll be pretty pleased myself."

The Professor was back from town when we arrived home, and tea that afternoon was almost a party. Alexander came with us, and over tea and toast and fish paste and crumpets, we talked and laughed as we pondered the whole story. I was so relieved I was almost giddy. Now I wouldn't have to wonder whether someone was following me, or have that uneasy sense that I was being watched. Now I could get on with life.

"Poor Beale must be quite mad," said the Professor. "Yet he had a fine mind once. Unfortunately, this research of his had become an obsession, and he was prepared to abduct you, Verity, and I suppose keep you a prisoner... He thought he was going to astonish everyone with this book of his, his *magnum opus*. And now I expect he'll be confined somewhere for the rest of his life."

"Poor man," said Judith.

"You're too soft-hearted," said Alexander.

"No, I'm not," she said. "Don't you think it's tragic, when a person builds his life around something that's not real and lets it destroy him?"

"Perhaps it is tragic," said Alexander. "But don't feel sorry for him. He was prepared to break the law. To harm, even to kill if necessary, for what he wanted. Wanting something that much can make you very strong, Miss Plush."

It was only after Alexander left that I realized we'd left the butterflies at the police station, and missed our appointment with Miss Love.

19

ALARMS AND ACCIDENTS

The next day SP sent Miss Love a telegram, apologizing for missing our appointment, and saying we'd call at two the following day. SP was eager to talk to Miss Love, and to see the list of people ("leads", they were called in the Confidential Inquiry business) that she'd promised to prepare for us. Though I have to confess that the whole thing didn't seem so urgent now that Dr Beale had been put away. I said as much to SP.

"But don't you want to know who you are, Verity?" he asked.

Well, I did know who I was. I was me, Verity Sparks: ex-apprentice milliner, assistant confidential inquiry agent and possible *septième étoile*. For all that it was exciting to think that out there, somewhere, were sisters and aunts and cousins – a whole family, in fact – I couldn't help hanging back just a little. The Plushes seemed like my family now.

Mrs Costello was not there to greet us this time, and Ivy timidly waved us upstairs. Daniel knocked and knocked, but there was no answer. I called through the keyhole. Still no answer, so we trooped back downstairs, and SP asked Ivy if Miss Love had gone out.

"No, sir."

"Did she come down for her breakfast this morning?"

"No, sir."

"Did she come down for her evening meal last night?"

"No, sir." Ivy's voice was getting fainter and fainter.

"When was the last time you actually saw Miss Love?"

"May I know why you ask?" came Mrs Costello's genteel tones. Her eyes shifted from my face to SP's, then to Daniel's and finally to poor Ivy's.

"They was just axing after Miss Minnie," whispered Ivy.

"And, what, pray, did you reply?"

"I was telling them she'd not come down last night."

"Didn't you send someone up to see if she was ill?" asked Daniel with an angry gleam in his eye.

"The missus said I was not to."

All eyes were back on Mrs Costello. She jangled

her keys, and said, "I give our boarders their privacy, which is what they require. But if you gentlemen are worried, I will escort you upstairs. Ivy! Get back to the scullery. I'll sort you later, my girl."

Mrs Costello knocked, as we had done, and then put the key in the lock. It turned, but the door didn't open.

"Let me try," said SP, and gave it a push. "Something is in the way. Help me, Opie."

The two of them gave the door one mighty shove, and the something rolled aside. It was Miss Minnie, lying on the floor so still that at first I thought she was dead.

"Miss Minnie! Wake up." Daniel gently shook her by the shoulder. She gave a little snort and then her head lolled sideways again.

"Dead drunk," said Mrs Costello. "Disgusting." She flounced out of the room.

Pot meet kettle, I thought, by the smell on *her* breath.

"I don't think she's drunk. I think she's unwell," said Daniel. "Look how pale she is."

"I'll go for the doctor," said SP. "Find a shawl, Verity, to keep her warm until I get back."

Easier said than done in the clutter of Miss Love's room.

"Perhaps that quilt will do," suggested Daniel. "Over there, on the sofa."

As I reached for it, something crunched under my feet. Macaroons. There was a half-eaten box of them on one of the side tables, and a broken plate and a few more of them scattered on the floor. It looked as if she'd been eating her favourite treat and suddenly keeled over. Poor Miss Minnie.

In less than quarter of an hour, SP came back with a doctor, a young fellow called Dr Raverat. His suit was shabby, his medical bag was battered, and his old watch was tied to a length of ribbon, but it seemed he knew his business.

"She has a pulse, but it's faint and very slow," he said. "I'd say she's had an overdose of some opiate drug. Most probably laudanum."

Laudanum was a medicine made of opium and alcohol, easy to buy and cheaper than gin. Madame used it when she felt a headache coming on.

"Will she recover?" asked Daniel.

"Yes," said the doctor. "But it's a good thing you and your friends came when you did."

"What is to be done for her now, sir?" I asked.

"She will need careful watching and nursing. If I might suggest…" He hesitated. "My wife and I have lodgings close by. Mrs Raverat is a good nurse."

"Bless you." SP took his hand and shook it heartily. "However can we thank you? Here's my card, and here's…" He felt in his breast pocket and brought out a couple of banknotes. "Will that do?"

"It will more than do, Mr Plush."

Daniel picked Miss Minnie up in his arms as if she'd been a child, and we made a procession down the stairs and through the hall to the front door. That's where Mrs Costello stopped us. She didn't seem in the least bit worried to see Miss Love carried down as floppy as a ragdoll. What worried her was next week's rent.

"Oh, for goodness sake," snapped SP, losing his usual good humour. "The rent shall be paid. Can't you see that Miss Love needs medical attention?"

Ivy crept out from the dining room and stroked Miss Minnie's hand.

"Poor little lady," she said. "She was so 'appy the other day when——" But Mrs Costello shut her up and started on about the rent again. We left.

Miss Minnie's collapse went right out of my head the moment we got back to Mulberry Hill. The Professor, wild-eyed and waving a piece of paper, met us at the door.

"What's happened?" asked SP. "What's wrong?"

"A telegraph boy has just been. It's a message from Penrose's Hotel in St Aubyn, where Almeria's staying," he said. "She's had a terrible accident – they don't say what it was – but she's sent for us. She wants us to come at once."

"Father." SP put his arm around the Professor, and for a few seconds the two of them clung together.

Mrs Cannister bustled in, looking suitably serious, with a copy of Bradshaw's Railway Directory in her hand.

"Professor, there's a train from King's Cross at ten o'clock tonight. It's a sleeper, and you would arrive before noon."

"Thank you, Mrs Cannister," he said. "I'll pack at once. Where's Judith?"

"Next door," supplied Etty, who was now also hovering in the hall. "The poor lady's near the end."

"So soon?"

"I'll go and get her," I said.

Now that there was no Dr Beale lurking about, I was happy to run down through the back garden and across the bridge to Mr Tissot's. Amy trotted along beside me, snuffling through the leaves, and I remembered that only a few weeks ago the trees were all golden and red with autumn colour. Now they were bare, the pond was choked with dead leaves and the terrace where we'd sat in the sunshine was damp and cold.

Mrs Anderson, the Scottish housekeeper, let me in. Her face was blotched red from crying and, without speaking, she gestured towards the drawing room. Mr Tissot and Judith were standing by the French windows, looking out at the dreary terrace and listening to a tall fat man in a black suit. They didn't see me come in, but the Savinovs did. Alexander and his father were sitting by the fire, and they came straight up to me. With a smile, Alexander took both my hands in his and kissed them. He was very like his father, I thought.

"I heard about your adventures," said Mr Savinov. "Thank God my son was there to help you."

"I think that Miss Sparks could have handled him quite well on her own."

"A young girl. She should not have to." Mr Savinov sounded angry. "The man is a lunatic. I hope they lock him up and throw away the key." He shook his head, as if to get rid of thoughts of Dr Beale, and then gestured towards the others. "The doctor says it is just a matter of keeping her comfortable now, that is all. To think that only a few weeks ago…" He didn't finish. Only a few weeks ago she was full of laughter and mischief, and now, like the leaves, she was dying.

"I need to speak to Judith," I said. She looked so tired and strained that I scarcely wanted to add to her troubles with the news about her aunt.

"Is something wrong?" asked Alexander.

At that moment, Judith turned.

There was no way to put it gently. "Mrs Morcom has been in an accident, Judith," I said. "She's asking for you."

Poor Judith. Back at Mulberry Hill, the Professor showed her the telegram and the railway timetable, and she ran upstairs to pack. Then straightaway she came back down.

"I feel torn in two, Father," she said. "Kathleen needs me. I can calm her. She frets and cries, and worries about Mr Tissot, but I can soothe her." Tears began to run down her cheeks. "I don't know what to do," she wailed. "Aunt wants all of us to be there, but … but…"

"Stay with Kathleen," said the Professor, suddenly decisive. "Stay with her tonight, and we will send word tomorrow. If need be, you can catch a train the following day. I pray the situation won't be that desperate."

"What about Verity?" said SP. "We have forgotten all about Verity. If you and I go to Cornwall, Father, and Judith stays with Kathleen, that will leave Verity here by herself."

"Not by myself at all," I said. "Mrs Cannister is here, and Cook, and the maids, and John in the coach-house, and O'Brien and Ben in the cottage."

"I never knew we kept so many staff," said the Professor with a strained smile.

"I will be perfectly all right," I said. "After all, there's no Dr Beale to worry about now."

Judith packed an overnight bag, and returned to the Tissots'. The Professor and SP went with her. When they came back, red-eyed the pair of them, they finished packing and ordered the carriage.

Cleopatra and her eggs were the only problem. SP had explained to me earlier that hatching eggs in captivity was a tricky business, for snakes are cold-blooded and produce no body heat of their own. In the wild, whenever Cleopatra felt herself cooling down, she'd leave her eggs, bask in the sun on a hot rock to bring her temperature back up, and then coil around the eggs again.

"The best we can do," he said, "is to put some river stones by the fire to heat, and then wrap them in cloth and put them into the case. I can't ask any of the staff to do it; they all insist on being terrified of the snakes, no matter how often I explain that they're

229

quite harmless. Do you think you can do it, Verity?"

"Of course I can," I said, acting more confident than I was. But with Judith nursing Kathleen, and who-knew-what wrong with Mrs Morcom, the least I could do was manage Cleopatra and her eggs.

20

A STRANGE CONVERSATION

I went up to my room at about ten o'clock. I put on my nightgown and dressing-gown, but since I had to stay up until eleven o'clock to give Cleopatra her hot rock, I couldn't go to bed. I don't think I would have slept, anyway. I kept thinking about Kathleen. How cruel this horrible disease was. She was kind-hearted and laughing. It wasn't fair.

I thought about the Professor and SP too, and wondered what they would find at Penrose's Hotel. They'd sent a couple of telegrams before they left, asking for more news, but no replies had come. It was the not knowing that was such a worry.

I sat on the hearth rug, hugging my knees and staring at the fire. "You never know what's round the corner," Cook would have said. Cook had a saying for every occasion. "You never know when your time is up," was another of them. It seemed Kathleen's time had come. What about Mrs Morcom? And poor Miss Love? Thinking about Miss Love led me on to Mrs Vic, and *la Belle Sauvage*, and Mrs Miller, and the medallion with the seven stars. I fingered the lucky piece and wondered once again about the six aunts and six sisters and—

Suddenly, I had a jolt to the chest. My fingers and hands itched and trembled, and I saw in front of me a woman with grey hair and a hooked nose, just staring out into nothing. In spite of the shock I recognized her at once. I'd seen her in Miss Minnie's album. It was Mrs Vic.

"*Mon Dieu,*" she whispered. "*Ce n'est pas possible. Il n'est pas ... Lyosha? Oh, non, non...*" Then she was talking, quickly and urgently, in accented English. "Lizzie, thank you! You are an angel, *chérie*. You are the only one I can trust. You mustn't tell a soul, not even your good Thomas ... no one. No one, you understand? Monsieur will be back at the end of the month, and I'll come then."

And my mother's voice, saying softly, "She's beautiful, Mrs Vic. She's so beautiful."

Mrs Vic faded, and I felt sick and shaky. I huddled closer to the fire and looked at the lucky piece. I'd tried to "read" it before, and got nothing. So why, all unexpected, had it happened this time?

And what did it mean?

"Monsieur will be back at the end of the month," she'd said. "And I'll come then…" She'd died before she could come and take me back. Monsieur? I knew that was French for "sir". Was Monsieur my father? That fitted in with the *septième étoile* story. But what else had she said? The only other French word I recognized was "no".

I was really cold now, so I put a few lumps of coal on the fire. Then I remembered. Cleopatra! Taking the candle, I went to do my duty.

I passed Mrs Cannister's room. The door was open, and she was in her armchair with the gas light still on. She was snoring, quite loudly, and her fire had gone out. I went in and tapped her lightly on the arm, but she just mumbled something and snored on. She'd knocked her night-time cup of cocoa onto the floor, and there was a trail of sticky brown liquid on her apron. She must have been exhausted, poor thing. There'd been so much to do, getting SP and the Professor off to catch their train. I turned the gas down so the room was dim, and tiptoed out.

The gas was still burning in the hall, and I wondered about that. Usually all the gas jets were turned off when the servants went to bed, but everything had been in an uproar today, so no wonder if the household was topsy-turvy. I would turn them down on my way back upstairs, I decided.

Antony was in his case in the conservatory, but Cleopatra had been put in Mrs Morcom's studio, and the room was hot, stale and stuffy from having a fire all day. I held my candle to the glass, and there she was, coiled around her six precious eggs.

I knew I had to be careful not to disturb her. She had no venom, of course, so her bite couldn't kill; it would just hurt a bit, like being scratched by a cat. Or so SP said. Nothing to be frightened of.

All the same, I was trembling as I raised the lid of her case. She stayed still as a statue, so I propped it open, removed the rock, put it down and shut the lid again. She stirred but didn't uncoil, thank goodness, for I don't know how I'd have dealt with a restless python on my own. I nudged the hot rock out from the hearth with the poker and wrapped it up.

"Bother," I said to myself. Now I'd have to prop the lid open again in order to get the new rock in. I fumbled it, and made a noise, and Cleopatra raised her triangular face and flicked her tongue at me. "Tasting the air," SP called it. Snakes don't have noses, so they smell with their tongues. I just hoped I didn't smell too good.

I'd placed the hot rock in the case without a bite when I heard a noise. Footsteps were coming towards me through the conservatory.

"Is that you, Mrs Cannister?" I called. There was no answer, and I called again. "Mrs Cannister?"

No answer, but a figure loomed in the doorway. In the dim and shadowy light it took a few seconds for me to work out who it was.

"Alexander." My heart was thumping so hard it hurt. "You frightened me."

"So sorry." He sketched a bow. "But I wouldn't have thought there was much that could frighten the intrepid Verity Sparks."

I felt a bit cross. "Well, you did," I said. A thought struck me. He must have come from Mr Tissot's, and a visit like this in the middle of the night could only mean one thing. "Kathleen." I faltered. "Is she...?"

"Kathleen?" he repeated in a puzzled voice. "Ah, Kathleen. There is no change."

"Oh," I said. Now it was my turn to be puzzled. "I thought you must have come to tell me she had passed away."

"No."

"Did Judith send you for something?"

"Miss Judith? Yes, yes, she did." But he didn't say what. He moved forward to warm his hands by the fire. "My mother died young too, you know."

He seemed different tonight. Odd. I wondered whether Kathleen's illness was affecting him more than he knew. "This must make you very sad," I ventured.

"Not terribly. I was only a baby when she died, and I don't remember her. Papa was both mother and father to me. You have lost both parents, Verity?" He sat down on one of the armchairs.

"Yes. My adopted parents." There seemed no harm in confiding in Alexander. I sat in the other chair. "I don't know who my real parents are, but we are on the case, as SP would say."

"And have you got very far?"

"No. We're at a bit of a standstill." I had a sudden idea. "Do you speak French, Alexander?"

"Yes. Why do you ask?"

"Can you tell me what this means?" I repeated what Mrs Vic had said. I spoke slowly, faltering a bit, but I knew I had it right.

"*Mon Dieu.*"

"My God." He sounded amused.

"*Ce n'est pas possible. Il n'est pas...*"

"It's not possible. He's not..."

"*Lyosha. Oh, non, non.* That's no, no. Is that right?"

"That's right."

236

"And what does *Lyosha* mean?"

He was looking at me very strangely. "It's a name, Verity. A nickname. Where did you hear it?"

"It's just something someone overheard," I said, getting up. "Something to do with one of our investigations. It doesn't make much sense."

"But it will, Verity. It will."

Alexander was staring at me now, and I didn't like the look on his face.

"Sit down, Verity. I am going to tell you a story. Actually, that's why I came here tonight."

Alexander was acting so oddly, and I started to wonder if he'd had too much to drink. "Perhaps tomorrow," I said.

"Once upon a time," he began, ignoring me, "there was a little boy and his father. There was no mother, no sisters or cousins or aunts to get in the way, and they were everything to each other. And then the father married again. The woman he married hated the boy."

I put my hand to my chest where the lucky piece, under my nightgown, suddenly felt hot against my skin. I had the strangest feeling: dizzy, and yet clear-headed at the same time. I could see the boy, like a picture in my mind. Solemn, pale, with white-blond hair falling over his forehead. It was Alexander.

"The boy was very unhappy. It was never like that before, when it was just the boy and his father."

I heard shouting. The boy crying. Doors slamming. Then the boy was older: not solemn now, but sad. And angry.

"Then something happened. The stepmother had a baby. A girl. The father doted on the baby. The boy loved the baby too, for she was very sweet, but he decided that if he was ever to be happy again—"

The baby was wrapped up, sleeping, in a lacy shawl. All I could see of her were dark eyelashes and fat pink cheeks. She was in the boy's arms, but I knew... My hands began to tingle. *I knew she was in danger.*

"No!" I cried. "Don't hurt her."

Alexander stopped, and I shivered, in spite of the warmth of the room. In the shadowy light from the fire and the lamp, his face looked like another person's. Harder, colder.

"It's just a story, Verity," he mocked.

I was trembling. "You're the boy."

"Yes, Verity. Clever Verity. Of course the boy is me. I didn't hurt her. I wrapped her up and took her miles away, near the river, and left her at the docks. But the old woman, the stepmother's nurse, was always creeping and spying and poking her nose in.

She followed me and found the baby. There was a bit of fuss about that, I can tell you." He gave a chuckle, for all the world like a naughty child.

I put my hand to my chest again. The lucky piece was burning and that familiar tingle was prickling and itching my fingertips. I thought my heart would knock its way out of my chest. Beneath his smiles and fine manners, Alexander was still that angry, sad boy, jealous of his father's love. Jealous of his father's new wife, and his own half-sister. So jealous, that he…

"Shall I go on?"

"No, you're frightening me."

Tingle, prickle, itch. What were my fingers trying to tell me? I hadn't lost anything. I wasn't trying to read an object. I tried to get up, but Alexander took hold of my wrists and forced me back down onto the chair.

"Don't be frightened," he said, but every nerve in my body jangled with fear as he touched me.

"Don't." I struggled against his grip. "Mrs Cannister! Etty!"

He laughed. "Don't bother with that. No one can hear you. Don't you want to know how the story ends?"

"No. Let me go."

"Shh. Listen. I wasn't going to harm her. But the

old nurse and the stepmother were so nasty to me, so horrible – they were going to tell my father such awful lies about me when he got back. I had to do it. Can't you see that? I had to."

"What did you do?" I whispered, but I already knew. Miss Minnie Love's album floated before my eyes. *Tragedy Strikes Twice at Prima Donna's Mansion.*

"The stepmother couldn't sleep. She could never sleep. And she used drops – knock-out drops, she called them. She drank water at bedtime too. Warm water and honey and lemon, every night, for her precious throat. So I put lots and lots of drops in her honey water and she didn't wake up. Then I thought, what if they find out about the drops? What if they can tell I gave them to her? So I started a fire in her bedroom. I did a good job too. Brought the whole second floor of the house crashing down. There was almost nothing left."

"You killed Isabella Savage," I said. "You killed the baby."

"Oh, that was the problem. The baby wasn't dead. The nosy Frenchwoman had taken her and given her to a friend. To keep her safe, she said, the interfering old crow. She shouldn't have told me that. It was silly of her." Alexander chuckled. "Well, I pushed her down the stairs. That showed her."

That showed her. He said it as if he was just a mischievous boy playing a trick. I stared at him, wondering where handsome, charming Alexander Savinov had gone. He'd murdered Isabella and Mrs Vic, and he'd tried to murder the baby as well.

Ah! Suddenly I saw.

"What is it, Verity Sparks? Have you only just worked it out?"

"I was the baby, wasn't I?" I was the baby Mrs Vic had given to her friend from the opera. I was the child of Isabella Savage and Pierre Savinov. I was Alexander's half-sister.

"You were always there, in the back of my mind. *Where is she? Where is she?* It kept me awake at nights, thinking that one day you might just pop up from nowhere, and expect your share."

"My share of what?"

"Of everything," Alexander said angrily. "Papa is quite rich, you know. Finding you was such a stroke of luck. You see, I'd employed Maxine – that's Madame Dumas – to keep an eye on Papa. I didn't want him to do anything silly, like get married and have children. She used to go to seances and spiritualist meetings with him, and after a while she realized that such gatherings were a useful way to obtain information about people. Wealthy people, grieving, eager for some message from the beyond. Often they would spill their secrets to a pretty, sympathetic Frenchwoman, and there might follow perhaps a bit of blackmail from time to time. I didn't care what she did, as long as Papa remained single. I'd told Maxine about my lost sister. Not the whole story, of course – women are so stupidly sentimental – and so that night at Lady Skewe's when Mrs Miller said '*La Belle Sauvage*', Maxine was immediately alert. She hurried straight to my rooms to tell me. It was interesting, I thought. It was worth keeping an eye on you. But then she described to me a little medallion you wore. Silver, with a design of seven stars... I had to act."

My hand crept to my neck. "The lucky piece."

"Give it to me," he ordered, holding out his hand.

I didn't even think of refusing.

"Ah," he said slowly, tracing the design with his forefinger. "I know that medallion well. It got me into a lot of trouble once. Isabella was silly and superstitious. She thought that if she wore this on the opening night, the opera would be a success. So I took it. I took it, and she was beside herself. How I laughed. But I wasn't careful enough; I kept it. I hid it in my room and the old crow found it. I should have thrown it down a drain so it was lost forever." He tossed it back to me. "Keep it. I've had my luck out of it. Thanks to Maxine and her sharp eyes, it led me to you." He lowered his voice and, deep and smooth as black velvet, said slowly, "Miss Sparks, I presume?"

I began to tremble. That nightmare voice in the dark. Foreign, but not quite. A gentleman's voice, and yet...

"It was you, not Dr Beale, who chased me that night after the seance."

"Yes, Verity, it was. I wanted to talk to you." He chuckled, and the sound of it nearly froze the marrow in my bones. He hadn't wanted to talk to me. He'd wanted to kill me. And now he was going to finish the job.

"Alexander, no." I tried to get out of the chair again but he hit me, hard, across the face.

"You need to understand," he said. "This is something I must do. Don't make it difficult."

"Please..."

My chair was directly in front of Cleopatra's case, and I hadn't put the lid back on. I sensed rather than heard the movement of air and the slide of scales on scales. Unseen, behind me, Cleopatra was beginning to uncoil from her eggs and rise up out of the case. I felt her against my back. Her head was on my shoulder.

SP had warned me never to let Cleopatra get

around my neck. Not that I would, of course, since she was a ruddy great python, not a fur stole. "She wouldn't mean to," he'd told me. "She doesn't think you're food – far too big – but she could squeeze too hard." Remembering that, I ducked my head to one side, and stood up out of her way.

I know I did faint the first time I met Cleopatra, but that was nothing compared to Alexander's reaction. He jumped up. He clutched at his chest and made a noise like he was choking, forming words but not able to speak. He took a couple of steps backwards and stumbled on something.

I swear that when I came through the conservatory Antony was safely in his case. But there he was, all six feet of him, sliding across the floor of the studio behind Alexander. Alexander looked down at what he had tripped on and screamed. Then he ran. He ran back through the dark conservatory, knocking over the cane furniture and pots, crashing into the raised beds, crunching through the ferns. Then I heard another noise. It was glass being shattered and smashed to smithereens. Then a long, hoarse cry.

I remember stumbling through the conservatory. I saw the broken glass too late, and cut my feet, but at the time I scarcely felt pain. There was enough of a moon to see Alexander lying on the tiled floor. He was still alive then, clutching his hand to his chest and gasping for breath. I cradled him in my arms. What else could I do? He said only one thing before he died.

"Veroschka."

I don't remember anything else after that.

21

THE TRUTH ABOUT
VERITY SPARKS

Judith told me what happened.

Kathleen died at dawn. The housekeeper made them a pot of tea and poured some brandy, and then Mr Savinov offered to escort Judith back home. She was near to dropping, for she'd had a hard few days and a long, long night.

It was a crisp morning. The dead leaves, powdered with frost, crackled under their feet, and early birds scattered and flew away as they passed. Judith drew deep, shuddering breaths as she walked, and Mr Savinov held her by the arm, repeating half to himself, half to her. "It will pass. It will pass."

They were puzzled when they got to Mulberry Hill, for they found none of the servants were up. No fires had been lit. The gas jets were still burning in the hall.

"What's this?" said Judith. It looked like red ink, or sealing wax. There were spots of it on the hall carpet, and on the stairs. And then more than spots, and smears of the stuff, long dribbles, and footprints. Mr Savinov knelt and touched his fingertip into the red. He sniffed it.

"This is blood," he said. Then, "Blood!" he shouted, and bounded up the stairs, taking them two or three at a time, calling my name.

I didn't hear him, of course. They found me in my room, curled up in front of a dead fire, with blood on my feet where they had been cut by broken glass. They thought I was dead too.

It wasn't till a fortnight later that I was able to sit up in bed for the first time. Judith plumped up my pillows and settled a shawl around my shoulders and SP put a pile of illustrated magazines beside me on the night table. The Professor brought in a bunch of hothouse roses and even Mrs Morcom (who said she couldn't abide a sick room) peeped around the doorframe to say hello.

"Dr Raverat says that what with the shock, and being chilled to the bone, you're lucky to have escaped with high fever and delirium," said SP.

"And no permanent damage to the respiratory

system, the heart or the brain," the Professor added cheerily.

"And if you can't remember anything for a time, Dr Raverat said not to worry. It's nature's way of healing, he said, with forgetfulness and rest." Judith stroked my hand.

"I do remember up until Alexander…" I began, and stopped.

SP hesitated. "You may as well know now. It seems that Antony and Cleopatra frightened him so much that he ran through the conservatory and straight into the glass door. Pierre confirmed that Alexander was terrified of snakes. Apparently, he had a weak heart, and … well, he died of fright. There wasn't a scratch on him."

"What happened afterwards?" I asked.

Rather a lot, it seemed. For one thing, Mrs Morcom came home, accompanied by SP and the Professor. The only accident she'd had was meeting up with an old school friend she'd always disliked. The telegram from Penrose's Hotel? There was no such place. The telegram was a trick of Alexander's, to get the family away from the house.

Inspector Grade turned up with the butterflies we'd left at the police station, and the news that while Dr Beale had indeed written the poison-pen letters and stalked me, he'd been at a Phrenology Colloquium at Oxford University on the night of the seance. So that was Alexander too. But of course I already knew.

Doctor Raverat and the inspector then worked out that the selection of treats – Dutch cocoa, sugared almonds and chocolate biscuits – which had been delivered to the Mulberry Hill servants with a note of thanks from the Professor, were also a trick of Alexander's. They were laced with Doctor Dearborn's Relaxation Remedy – laudanum, in other words. Luckily for them, the dose was designed to make them sleep. Not so Miss Minnie. Alexander had intended the drugged macaroons to kill her, so she couldn't give us the names of anyone who knew of the friendship between Mrs Vic and my mother.

"So the mystery is quite cleared up," I said to the Plushes.

"As much as it will ever be," said the Professor. "And Verity, my dear, there is someone waiting downstairs who would dearly love to see you. It is Pierre Savinov. May he come up?"

I nodded.

"We will leave you two together, then."

Mr Savinov came into my room slowly, like an old

man, and sat heavily on the chair by the bed. He took my hand.

"Thank God," was all he could say for a long time. Tears ran down his cheeks, and he ignored them. "Thank God."

"I'm so sorry," I whispered. "I'm so sorry about Alexander."

"He is better off where he is. He can be at peace," said Mr Savinov. And then he told me the last of the tale.

"Alexander – Lyosha, I called him – was always different," he said. "Perhaps it was because he never had a mother or a real home. Anna – my first wife, poor soul – also had a weak heart. She died when he was a baby. After that we led a wandering sort of life, just the two of us. I sometimes think he was happier when we were poor. He was always passionately attached to me. I knew he was not happy when Isabella and I married. But when you came, he spent hours hanging over your cradle and smiling, singing, making faces. Isabella and I were so relieved. He called you Veroschka – that means 'little Vera'. I was in Amsterdam on business at the time of the fire. He was so distressed that he could not save Isabella and the baby."

Oh. So Mr Savinov did not know that Alexander had started the fire.

"You remember Madame Dumas? You met her at the seance. Maxine is her name. She told me the truth the day after Alexander's death. I thought Maxine was my friend, but it seems Alexander had hired her to … to keep an eye on me." He sighed. Poor Mr Savinov. "By profession, Maxine is, like our Professor Plush, an investigator. But without the integrity of that fine gentleman, alas.

"This is the story that Alexander told Maxine. I don't know if it is true or not, and now I will never know. It was well known that Victoire had the second sight. She must have had some kind of premonition, for on the night of the fire she took you to be looked after by a friend, without telling Alexander. After the fire, she told him you were saved, but then … her accident.

"Alexander was ill when I returned from abroad. Brain fever, they called it. I thought I would lose him too. It was a terrible time. He lost his memory for a while, and when at last he regained it, he did not want to distress me by raising false hopes about the baby being alive." He shrugged his shoulders. "At least that is what he told Maxine. For years he had been searching for you. You see, he needed to find you because you were the rightful heiress to Isabella's money."

This was news to me. "Money?"

He sighed. "The Parker Pork fortune. Isabella's family were in the meat-packing business in Canada. I was doing well enough when we married, but when Isabella died, her inheritance came to me and I became very, very rich. Everything I owned – my money, Isabella's money – would have been Alexander's when I died. Oh, Alexander… He knew that somewhere in the world Vera Savinov was alive and the Parker Pork millions were hers, all right and tight, as you British would say. It seems that the thought of it ate away at him. Greed? That old jealousy of his? I cannot tell. It seems I did not know my son."

Should I tell him the truth? Now was the time to do it. But somehow I couldn't. Mr Savinov already knew his son was wicked. Surely, he did not need to know everything.

The moment passed, and he began talking about his wife, Isabella. My mother.

"Beautiful, talented, temperamental…" He was lost in thought for a few seconds. "She could have lived a life of a lady of fashion. But she had a voice, such a voice. Her talent could not be denied. She went to Paris and later Milan – that was where she had her first success, in *La Gioconda*. By then she'd changed her name to Isabella Savage – a better name for a diva than Penny Parker, no? Always her old nurse, the faithful Victoire, went with her. Her brother insisted."

"Brother? Surely she had sisters? Six sisters? Wasn't she the seventh daughter?"

"No. There was one brother, Hiram. What makes you think she had sisters?"

"This," I said. I slipped the silk cord from around my neck and handed him the lucky piece and the ring.

"My mother's wedding ring! Isabella and I always meant you to have it when you yourself..." He stared at it. Where was it taking him, I wondered? To happy times, to love and weddings, a little baby girl... "And the *amulette*! The lucky stars."

I could hold back no longer. "Don't you know that it's the sign of the seventh − of the *septième étoile* − the seventh daughter of a seventh daughter? I have the gift, you see. Miss Lillingsworth is sure I must be one."

"It was Victoire's," he said in a puzzled voice.

"Victoire's?" All my castles in the air vanished into nothing. No aunts, no sisters, no cousins. No explanation for my itchy fingers.

"Yes," he said. "It was a ritual with Isabella and Victoire, that she should always wear it hidden beneath her costume on the first night of a new opera."

"So Victoire was one of seven sisters?"

"I don't know. Is it so important?"

I shook my head. "It's nothing."

Mrs Vic may indeed have been a *septième étoile*, but I wasn't. Miss Lillingsworth was wrong. My gifts were lucky, that's true, but the luck was mine alone.

"She must have left the charm and the ring with you when she took you to Mrs Sparks. Which one it was that kept you safe, I do not know."

But I did. I silently thanked Mrs Vic for saving my life. Mr Savinov held the ring and the lucky piece in his large palm as if they were fairy gold and likely to melt away any second.

"Keep them," I said. "They're as much yours as mine."

I was happy for him to have them. Although Isabella Savage had given birth to me, Ma was and ever would be my real mother. I had a fairy godmother too – Mrs Vic. But I didn't need a token to remember her by. Because she smuggled me out of the house and gave me to Ma, I had my life.

"Something good has come from all this sorrow," said Mr Savinov. "I have found you."

My lovely, lovely lion, with tragedy after tragedy in his life. I put out my hand timidly, all of a sudden feeling shy. "I have found my father."

Mr Savinov took my hand. "You know, Verity, in all my years of trying, I have never received one message, not one single message, from beyond the grave. From Isabella, who I loved so dearly, and who loved me ... not a word. It was Maxine and Alexander who led me to you, and so I forgive them. There is a Russian saying: 'After a storm comes fair weather; after sorrow comes joy.'" He kissed my hand. "You are my joy, Verity."

22

ENDINGS AND BEGINNINGS

It took me a few more weeks to get well. When I came downstairs for the first time, I realized that life had been going on without me. The Professor, Mrs Morcom, Judith and Daniel and SP were there, wearing paper hats and tinsel crowns. Toasts were being drunk. There was hugging and kissing and laughing all round.

"What is going on?" I asked.

"Daniel has proposed to Judith and she's accepted," said SP. "They are planning—"

"Well, I have plans too," Mrs Morcom interrupted, thumping her glass of Madeira down so hard that the wine splashed the tablecloth. "This place bores me to tears."

"Thank you, Almeria, and same to you," said the Professor.

She glared at him. "Not Mulberry Hill, Saddy.

England. So I have decided to travel to Australia on another painting tour."

Suddenly, they were all talking at once. Australia. Somewhere new, somewhere fresh. Somewhere a young man like Daniel Opie could make his mark.

"It's a young country," said Judith. "Here, everyone is judged by their pedigree, as if we were prize cows. But in Australia, no one cares who your great-grandfather was."

"No one dares tell," said Mrs Morcom, dryly. "Half of them were convicts."

"It just so happens," said the Professor, "that I was approached by a firm of lawyers today. A firm of lawyers from Halifax in Yorkshire. The improbably named Bustard, Hawk and Chaffinch. They have a client who wants the Confidential Agents to follow up a complex matter both here in London and in Australia. It could be a start for you, Daniel."

"Father!" protested SP, taking off his crown and throwing it at the mantelpiece. "Am I to be left out?"

"You may go, my boy, if that's what you want," said the Professor. "Do you good to have a change." He slapped his son on the shoulder, and SP grinned.

"But what about you, Professor?" I asked. "You'll be all alone here."

"Not at all," he said, sounding almost pleased.

"I have my club, and the SIPP, and plenty of friends, and of course, my research—"

"Waste of time," commented Mrs Morcom.

"Happy endings all round," said the Professor.

"No, happy beginnings," said SP. "After all, it's nearly 1879." He turned to me and took my hand very gently, as if aware that I was not part of this excitement. They'd all been very careful of me, like I was a china doll, since I'd been sick. "What are your New Year's plans, Verity?"

In the last year I'd been a milliner's apprentice, and then an assistant confidential inquiry agent, and now the rich Mr Savinov's long-lost daughter. I'd been stalked and nearly murdered. I'd thought I was a seventh star, and I'd found out I wasn't. I'd discovered who my real parents were, which made me love Ma and Pa all the more. My itchy fingers had led me to lost objects and dead people, and helped me to find the truth about myself. As I looked around the table – at the Professor and SP, at Judith and Daniel in a glow of new love, and at Mrs Morcom in her pink paper hat, I felt a little lost. Lost and left out.

I dearly loved Papa Savinov, but somehow the Plushes had become my family. The Professor must have known what I was feeling, for he said, "You may always come and stay here with me, Verity. Whenever you wish."

SP bounced to his feet. His eyes were sparkling. "Why don't you, Verity?" he said, taking my hand.

"Why don't I what?"

"Why don't you come to Australia with us? Why not?"

My Parker Pork fortune was to be held in trust for me until I was twenty-five, but I was to have a generous allowance, and Papa Savinov wanted me to come and live with him.

"But not here," he said. I was spending the day with him in his apartments at the Hotel Excalibur. "We will need a house somewhere very nice. Park Lane, Mayfair — too fashionable. Perhaps one of those so English leafy squares, Grosvenor or Chester," he mused.

"What about St John's Wood?" Then I could be near Mulberry Hill as well.

"No." He frowned. "That is not at all respectable for a young English lady such as you will be. And we will need room for a chaperone or a companion, and a lady's maid—"

"A chaperone? A companion? Whatever for?"

"I am away so often, in Paris or Moscow or Prague,

and for months at a time, my dear. Of course you will need someone."

"Can't I come with you?"

"Sometimes, perhaps."

I thought about what he'd said all day. I thought about it and thought about it, and eventually I knew what I must do.

"Papa Savinov," I said. We were sitting together in front of the fire. The hotel waiter had just brought us afternoon tea, and a stand with three tiers of little sandwiches and iced cakes stood on the table between us. He looked so contented, drinking Assam tea and planning a London house and a country place and a companion and a piano teacher and riding lessons and the rest of it – and here I was about to spoil it.

"Yes, Veroschka?"

"I told you that Mrs Morcom and Daniel and Judith and SP are all going to Australia, didn't I?"

"You did."

"I want to go to Australia too."

"Ah." He looked at me, long and sad, and gave a great big sigh.

I felt my heart would break for him, and quickly I said, "I'm sorry, Papa Savinov. If you really don't wish it, I won't go."

"You don't think you can be happy with me?"

"It isn't that. You're kind and good and I know I will have everything I want, but – but I don't like doing nothing, Papa. I can't be a lady. I can't sit around and pay calls and buy hats and embroider doilies."

"But I'd like you to be a lady, Veroschka. A real English lady. And who knows, one day perhaps to marry a gentleman. Imagine yourself – Lady Vera! Wouldn't you like that?"

"I'll never be a lady, Papa. Don't you see? It's like Miss Judith says, they've all got pedigrees like prize cows. They won't want me."

"But with your Parker Pork inheritance, *chérie*."

"Pooh to that," I said, snapping my fingers. "I know all about fortune hunters. Cook told us. I don't want someone to marry me just for my money. Papa, do you understand?"

He thought for a while, and finally said, "Yes. I do. There's nothing tame about you, Veroschka. I think you are rather like me. Always seeking adventures. You know, I have businesses and investments all over the world, but none in Australia." His eyes began to sparkle.

"You mean…?"

He nodded. "I would like very much to see this land so faraway and strange."

I gasped with delight and took his hands.

"You do not mind your old papa coming along?"

"Of course I don't." I kissed his grey lion's head. And a sudden thought struck me. I'm not one to rake over the past, wondering what would have happened if this or that had been different, but it was almost funny, wasn't it? To Lady Throttle I'd been a little nobody, just a milliner's apprentice. She'd thought she could use me in her dishonest scheme and then toss me away. But in a way she was responsible. For my friendship with the Plushes, for my fine clothes and comfortable bed, for this hotel room and the luxurious afternoon tea spread out on the table – and for my father.

"You know, Papa," I said. "We would never have found each other if that horrid Lady Throttle hadn't accused me of stealing her diamond."

"You are my diamond, cherie. My priceless, precious jewel. Lost for so many, many years..." He shuddered, and I snuggled up to him.

"But found now, Papa. Well and truly found."

ACKNOWLEDGEMENTS

I was awarded a Varuna Fellowship to work on this project and I'd like to thank Peter Bishop, Creative Director of Varuna, The Writers' House, for his encouragement. Thank you also to Mary Verney of Walker Books, whose careful and enthusiastic editing made *Diamonds and Deception* the best it could be.

And, as always, thanks to Howard and Lachie.

A MARY QUINN MYSTERY

⁓❧ May 1858 ❧⁓

A foul-smelling heat wave paralyzes London.
Mary enters a rich merchant's household to solve the
mystery of his lost cargo ships. But as she soon learns,
the house is full of deceptions, and people are not
what they seem – including Mary herself.

The first book in the riveting
Victorian detective trilogy

On the morning of the best day of her life,
Maud Flynn was locked in the outhouse singing
"The Battle Hymn of the Republic".

Plain, clever, impertinent Maud cannot believe
her luck when she is plucked from her dreary
existence at the Barbary Asylum for Female Orphans
and adopted by the wealthy Hawthorne sisters. But
life with her new guardians turns out to be quite
different from anything Maud could have imagined…

"People throw the world 'classic' about a lot, but
A Drowned Maiden's Hair genuinely deserves
to become one." *The Wall Street Journal*

Rob Lloyd Jones

WILD BOY

London, 1841. A boy covered in hair, raised as a monster, condemned to life in a travelling freak show. A boy with an extraordinary power of observation and detection. A boy accused of murder; on the run; hungry for the truth. Ladies and Gentlemen, take your seats. The show is about to begin!

"A pacey, atmospheric and thrilling adventure." *Metro*

WILD BOY AND THE BLACK TERROR

A new sensation grips London – a poisoner who strikes without a trace. Is there a cure for the black terror? To find out, Wild Boy and Clarissa must catch the killer. Their hunt will lead them from the city's vilest slums to its grandest palaces, and to a darkness at the heart of its very highest society.

"An exhilarating read with great characters."
The Bookbag

ABOUT THE AUTHOR

Susan Green lives in the historic gold-rush town of Castlemaine in Central Victoria, Australia with her husband, son and Gus the miniature schnauzer. She has been a teacher, radio producer, youth worker, cook and bookseller, but she knew she wanted to be a writer by the time she was eight years old. She has written twelve books for children and young adults. *Diamonds and Deception* is her first novel for Walker Books.